VIKING
Mystery
Suspense

REVENGE

OF THE

COOTIE

GIRLS

Also by Sparkle Hayter

What's a Girl Gotta Do?

Nice Girls Finish Last

Sparkle Hayter

REVENGE

OF THE

COOTIE

GIRLS

❈ ❈ ❈

VIKING

VIKING
Published by the Penguin Group
Penguin Books USA Inc., 375 Hudson Street,
New York, New York 10014, U.S.A.
Penguin Books Ltd, 27 Wrights Lane, London W8 5TZ, England
Penguin Books Australia Ltd, Ringwood, Victoria, Australia
Penguin Books Canada Ltd, 10 Alcorn Avenue,
Toronto, Ontario, Canada M4V 3B2
Penguin Books (N.Z.) Ltd, 182–190 Wairau Road,
Auckland 10, New Zealand

Penguin Books Ltd, Registered Offices:
Harmondsworth, Middlesex, England

First published in 1997 by Viking Penguin,
a division of Penguin Books USA Inc.

1 3 5 7 9 10 8 6 4 2

PUBLISHER'S NOTE
This is a work of fiction. Names, characters, places, and incidents
either are the product of the author's imagination or are used
ficitiously, and any resemblance to actual persons, living or dead,
events, or locales is entirely coincidental.

LIBRARY OF CONGRESS CATALOGING IN PUBLICATION DATA
Hayter, Sparkle, date.
Revenge of the Cootie Girls / Sparkle Hayter.
p. cm.
ISBN 0-670-86940-6
I. Title.
PR9199.3.H39R48   1997
813'.54—dc20   96-43984

This book is printed on acid-free paper.
(∞)

Printed in the United States of America
Set in Minion

To CJW

and

The Goils

Sandi Bill
Diana Greene
Marianne Hallett
"Weird Deirdre" Kirk
"Right Lisa" Mann
"Left Lisa" Napoli
Tamayo Otsuki
Andrea Peyser
Kathrine Piper
Alesia Powell
Annalee Simpson
Siv Svendsen
Eva Valenta
Lynn "E." Willis

and

my mom, Grace Jacqueline Audrey Bacon Hayter;
my sister, Sandra Dawn MacIntosh;
and my niece Jennifer Ann Hayter

※

Female friends are the greatest hazard in a working woman's life, for they cannot be casual.
—DAWN POWELL, 1944

Friendship is far more tragic than love. It lasts longer.
—OSCAR WILDE, "A Few Maxims for the Instruction of the Overeducated"

Readers of NANCY DREW need no assurance that the adventures of resourceful Louise Dana and her irrepressible sister Jean are packed with thrills, excitement, and mystery. Every girl will love these fascinating stories which tell how the DANA GIRLS, like Nancy Drew herself, meet and match the challenge of each strange new mystery.
—From the inside flap of *By the Light of the Study Lamp*, a Dana Girls mystery by Carolyn Keene, Copyright 1938, Grosset & Dunlap, Inc.

REVENGE

OF THE

COOTIE

GIRLS

❈ PROLOGUE ❈

BOY, IT'S HARD to believe now, but not long before the Girls' Night Out Fiasco, I was complaining about being bored.

All in all, my job was okay, my cautiously nonmonogamous love life was okay, nobody I knew had been murdered recently, my cat was making decent money as an advertising spokesfeline which I, as her accountant, embezzled freely, and my urge to walk the streets randomly slapping people silly had subsided.

That's when the attacks started.

Most people have panic attacks. Panic was a fairly normal state for me. I had boredom attacks. A voice would sound, *You have to do SOMETHING,* echoing like Poe's tell-tale heart. I suppose I was lucky it didn't say, "If you build it they will come," or, "Only you can save the dauphin from the English." Still, this was a voice that disturbed me, and since it didn't specify exactly what I should do, it sent me all over the place in search of boredom relief.

Over the course of the next few months, I tried shopping, massages, trendy scenes, drag balls, poetry slams, and sleeping with twenty-five-year-olds. Well, one twenty-five-year-old. But it was all too been-there-done-that. I tried working out my ennui in the employee gym, but, damn, exercise is boring. So repetitive. Everyone had suggestions about how to put the bounce back in my pounce, from bungee jumping to Prozac to magic herbs and candles to Kendo, the art of Japanese swordfighting. Nothing worked for very long.

Until, that is, I started meddling in the rich and interesting lives of my insane girlfriends. That's what got me mixed up with my neighbor Sally in the spring, prompted me to take on an intern in the Special Reports unit that fall, and led to the revival of Girls' Night Out, a semiregular frenzy of female bonding with whichever of my goilfriends was around. One thing leads to another, and another, and another. . . .

Girls' Night Out by definition wasn't about networking or consciousness raising or art appreciation or sensitive female bonding. It was about laughs, plain and simple. The whole idea was to go all night, being goofy and having fun, to "get silly," as Phil, my super, had advised me during my ennui. After a hard week doing budgets, managing people, being managed, raising kids, or investing zillions of dollars for clients, it's fucking Miller time, man.

In theory, at least. Maybe I was getting old. When I was younger, I'd go all night, from juke joint to juke joint, raising hell all over town. But every year it gets a little harder to do that.

My name is Robin Jean Hudson and I am the executive producer of the Special Reports unit at the prestigious All News Network, which sounds a lot more high-falutin' than it actually is. Though we try to do a few classy pieces every year, our bread and butter in Special Reports is UFO abductees, weird cults, crop circles, Satan, and abnormal sexual practices, sometimes all of the above at once.

Ever since my former boss, Jerry Spurdle, went to Berlin to be the bureau chief and avenge two world wars, I've been boss in the unit. As it turns out, I am good at bossing. Who knew? I am divorced, childless, and I live on New York's Lower East Side—excuse me, *East Village*—with my cat, Louise Bryant, of Aloof and Fussy Cat Food fame. She is part of their hero-cats ad campaign because she once saved my life, even though she didn't mean to. She was just pissed because she hadn't been fed.

Lately, I've been thinking about all the accidents, happy and otherwise, that send one's life spinning in a completely different direction. If my mother hadn't disobeyed her father back in 1957 and gone out with my dad in his dad's Packard to look for Sputnik in the night sky, I wouldn't even be here. I am very grateful to my mom and dad, and his dad, and the entire Soviet postwar space program, most of the time.

On top of all the accidents, there are the dozens, maybe hundreds, of decisions we make every day that have an impact on the future in ways big, small, minuscule.

For example, a simple thing like taking French in high school could have radically changed my life. I almost took French in high school, but at the last minute I changed my mind when I saw Doug Gribetz was signing up for Swedish. Since I had been in puppy love with Doug Gribetz since kindergarten, from the first time I looked up over my Lincoln Logs and saw him looking back, I decided to try Swedish as well, though I was too scared to speak to him in any language. After a week, he transferred out of Swedish. French was filled by then, so I stuck Swedish out for the semester, just barely passing. Nothing against our fine Scandinavian brothers and sisters, but Swedish is a language I can't speak without feeling goofy and cracking up, so I didn't learn very much. And I didn't go back to French until I was thirty and planning a vacation to Paris.

A little decision like that, and it made such a difference. But it wasn't just French, or boredom, or my bad-tempered cat, that facilitated the events of the last Girls' Night Out. There were a lot of twists and turns along the way that contributed. If my boyfriend Chuck hadn't forbidden me to go to the beach for spring break in 1979, things would have been different. If I hadn't been so docile with Chuck, I would have gone to the damned beach anyway.

And maybe I would have had more self-esteem and I wouldn't have been so docile, so grateful for Chuck's attention, if it wasn't for Mary MacCosham and the cooties.

Damn. That's a heavy thought. Because of cooties, lives were saved, and lives were lost.

❖ 1 ❖

NORMALLY, I feel a little thrill when I return to New York, which starts as the plane begins its descent into the airport and the little houses and gardens of Long Island and Queens come into view. It picks up steadily on the drive into the city and fully inflates when the skyline of Manhattan suddenly looms over the Calvary Cemetery in Queens. There's something about that juxtaposition of the gleaming skyline and the vast cemetery that almost always gets me where I live. I don't know why.

But that Halloween, the LaGuardia control tower kept my plane circling for over an hour, and after I'd seen the little houses for the twenty-seventh time the thrill was completely gone. The traffic on the ground was even worse, backed up all the way from the goddamned airport. The city/cemetery panorama was frozen in front of me for an hour, and lost its luster in about half that time.

It took one long, horn-slamming hour just to get to the midtown tunnel, and another forty-five minutes to get through it. By the time we got to the Manhattan side my cab driver, who had painfully observed the Taxi and Limousine Commission's new politeness guidelines when I got into the car, was banging his fist on the steering wheel and swearing like a longshoreman's parrot. I don't mean to throw stones, because I've employed the odd cussword or two when the occasion demanded it. In New York, cussing serves a healthy purpose, often venting and/or replacing anger. Better a sturdy Anglo-Saxon expletive that has stood the test of time than a punch in the nose, I always say.

But cussing wasn't helping this guy one bit.

"It's okay," I said, trying to calm him down.

"No, it's not okay," he said. "I have a curse on me!"

Why this curse was put upon him I never learned—he kept breaking off into his native language—but I did gather that an enemy had cursed him. And what a curse. Because of it, his face was changing into someone else's, his penis was receding into his body, and he couldn't seem to escape bad traffic.

Right, gotta go now, the microchip in my buttocks is beeping, I thought, but didn't say, though I generally believe one good insane comment deserves another.

Instead I said, "Everything will work out," because I was trying to be more mature and nurturing and all that, now that I was a semirespectable executive.

That's when he flipped.

"It will work out? I have a curse on me! How can it work out? I'VE HAD IT! This is the last straw!" he screamed. He threw his door open and took off running.

I sat there in the back seat, thinking he'd come back, you know. The guy picked a jim-dandy time to have a nervous breakdown. This crazy cabbie was even worse than the one who believed Korean greengrocers were involved in a conspiracy to spread rumors that he was homosexual.

Cars were honking behind me. For a split second there, I wanted to bolt screaming from the cab myself. But, no, I told myself, calm down. You're a problem-solving grownup. This obstacle can be overcome. I called the cab company on my handy cellular telephone.

The line was busy.

What choice did I have? Schlep my two big suitcases a mile to and from the subway? Not after the day I'd had. Find another cab? Ha! I had a better chance of finding Bob Dole in a Lollapalooza mosh pit than another free cab in a Manhattan traffic jam.

So, despite a longtime driving phobia, I got behind the wheel and I headed home, wondering, What else could possibly go wrong today?

You'd think, after everything I'd been through, I'd know the answer to that one, seeing as my life is ruled by only one immutable law: Murphy's.

The funny thing is, if I had been thinking with my genitalia instead of with my brain, I wouldn't have taken the cab from hell. At the airport, a nice-looking man offered to share his cab with me, but out of the corner of my eye I saw another cab coming up so I declined, thinking I'd save time and energy by taking my own cab. Instead of going back to Manhattan with a handsome and chivalrous companion, I rode back with a man under a curse who then deserted me in the trenches.

I would have thought it was some kind of sign or omen, except I no longer believed in that crap.

If you've ever driven in Manhattan you know what a rough ride it can be. There are no rigid traffic lanes, and traffic laws are considered to be optimistic suggestions rather than anything actually enforceable. You never know when the guy in the far-right lane next to you will abruptly decide to make a left-hand turn, or when someone will dart across the middle of the street. Pedestrians routinely cross against lights, leisurely taking their time even when they see a car coming. Most of the time, the cars don't even slow down, they just honk and trust the pedestrians will scatter in time. On my way home, I almost mowed over a blind woman and a man wheeling a shiny steel hot-dog wagon down the street.

Thank God other cabbies, seeing me struggling, let me cut in, and I was able to get to some clear space on Second Avenue. But, man, were my nerves were jangled when I finally pulled up to my apartment building on East 10th street on Manhattan's Lower East Side—excuse me, East Village. I felt real empathy for the AWOL cabbie.

After I unloaded my bags from the trunk and dragged them to the steps of my building, I stopped for a moment to catch my breath. As a rule, I like to get in and out of my building quickly to avoid my ancient neighbor Mrs. Ramirez, who is always trying to provoke me into a fist-fight. Due to a fairly strong societal taboo against elder abuse, I try my damnedest to avoid her. But, luckily, she was in Puerto Rico visiting her even more ancient mother, so I had the luxury of lingering on my stoop.

There is something calming about my street at this time of day. It was the blue hour, the hour after the sun sets and the sky begins to darken. There was just enough light left to illuminate the deep color of the sky and give the air around me a grainy texture and a blue tinge. The windows seemed milky and people on the street were starting to darken into silhouettes.

The days were getting shorter, but it was also unseasonably warm and humid for the end of October. We'd been having freak weather in New York for a couple, maybe three years. This, according to my neighbor Sally, was one of the signs of the coming apocalypse, though the people out on the street didn't seem to see anything ominous in the warm weather. There were a lot of people outside enjoying it, sitting on their stoops, yakking, playing music. Two men sat in folding chairs and watched a black-and-white television set on the hood of a low-slung car. The TV was tethered to a tenement apartment on the second floor by a series of extension cords.

Above them, a woman hung her head out a window and hollered for her kid, Ronnie. In the distance, another mother called her kids. It was dinnertime, and the mothers were calling their children in, like we were in some small town, not on the Lower East Side of Manhattan. My some-time boyfriend Mike once said it reminded him of Paki-stan, where muezzins in different mosques sing the evening call to prayer, first one, then another, then another, their overlapping songs echoing throughout the hills.

In about an hour the kids would all be out on the street again, extorting candy from people and doing God knows what, and the small-town resemblance would end. When I was their age, kids used to toilet-paper houses and go on undercover garden-gnome-switching operations on Hal-loween. But, then, unlike a lot of kids in my neighborhood, kids in my day didn't have guns, so our entertainment options were more limited. And we didn't get as much candy.

"Welcome back, luv," said my super, Phil, going out as I was going in. " 'Ow was your trip?"

"Great until today," I said, giving him the highlights. Even before the cursed cabbie, it had been a pretty shitty day. I'd been on the West Coast on business for my net-work and for Womedia, a women's service organization I had joined. I had to fly back via Denver, transferring planes, the second of which aborted its first takeoff because of an air-pressure problem, which was finally fixed with, according to passenger rumor, a piece of stick and duct tape. There was a crying baby on the flight from Denver, and the guy next to me complained about it in a stage whisper through clenched teeth the whole time. "Why doesn't she shut him up?" he said about 150 times, and, "They shouldn't allow babies on passenger planes." I al-most asked him how they were supposed to fly—in little carriers with the dogs and cats in freight? Crying babies don't annoy me for some reason, but guys who complain about them drive me up a wall.

"Well, at least your day 'asn't been boring," Phil said.

"I 'ear you saw your ex-'usband and 'is fiancee in L.A."

"Where did you 'ear that?" I said, imitating his working-class English accent.

"I hhhheard it on E! this afternoon," he said.

That's the problem with having a famous ex with a famous fiancée. Someone sees you with them at Spago and the next thing you know it's on the airwaves.

And what a great decision that was, staying an extra night in Los Angeles to have dinner with my ex and his beautiful fiancée, whom I liked, of course, because who wouldn't like an amusing, pretty, charming, and age-appropriate woman, and with her own career as an independent filmmaker to boot. Naturally, I was thrilled that Burke, my ex, was marrying this gem, and not, say, some semiliterate dullard in itchy clothes.

"Sometimes, luv, people are only meant to take each other partway in life," Phil said.

"Yeah, so I found out on the ride in from the airport."

"Mike going to be 'ere this weekend?"

"I don't know," I said. "He's supposed to call and let me know. If his shoot finishes early tonight, he's going to fly in, but if it goes late, he's going to stay in Arizona for the weekend. And either way is fine with me. I have a lot of work to do."

"What are you doing tonight?"

"Going out with the girls—Tamayo, Claire, my intern Kathy, and maybe Sally."

Our neighbor Helen Fitkis, unrepentant communist and widow, came out of the building and said, "I'm ready to go now, Phil. Hello, Robin."

"We're off to the movies, luv," Phil said. "Stop by tomorrow for tea."

"Okay," I said, and watched them walk off together. At first, I couldn't figure out what Phil and his new best friend

Helen Fitkis had in common. He was apolitical, she was as red as they come, though since Phil moved in she had calmed down a bit and stopped distributing her angry, monthly leaflets calling for a RENT STRIKE in big black letters. He was lighthearted, she came off as seriously humor-impaired. But they were contemporaries who both spoke Esperanto and remembered World War II. You could tell how well they got on just watching them walk, neither too fast nor too slow but at the same pace, easy and comfortable with each other.

Good, I thought, as I picked up my bags and went inside. Maybe it would turn into Love (or, as I know it, The Madness), and Phil would settle down here. The man had spent his peripatetic retirement working odd jobs all over the world to finance trips on his own nickel to work in refugee camps. He never stayed more than a year or two in any one place and he'd been in New York for more than a year now, most of that as our super. Recently he'd been seen with a Swahili grammar under his arm, a bad sign. Well, a bad sign for us, his neighbors, a good sign for Swahili-speaking refugees somewhere.

The first lucky break I got all day was a note on my door from Sally, the bald witch downstairs. "Robin," she wrote, "I fed Louise in the morning and stacked your mail in a box by your desk. I don't think I'll be able to join you tonight because of client business, but call me just in case I finish early. Sorry."

No apology necessary, I thought, with great relief.

"I had a dream and you were in it. An old woman was leading you towards the horizon. A man was there. I couldn't see his face," her note went on, adding that she was fairly certain her dream fit into my daily horoscope, which she had done as a Halloween present and enclosed. I read the first line, about how communication problems were going to figure into my day, and ignored the rest. I'd had my fill of nuttiness on the ride in from the airport.

If my new good luck held, she wouldn't catch up with me. Sally had been a very taxing friend, always in the midst of a Huge Crisis or else driving me nuts with her New Age chatter and her psycho-romantic fantasies about True Love (The Madness). She's one of those people who are always madly in love or madly looking for love, with often bad results (see Huge Crises, above).

Even though her own life was a mess and she'd take no advice from me, she insisted on telling me what she saw in my "future," and what I was supposed to be doing with *my* life, particularly my love life. Yeah, I'm going to take advice from a bald woman with a scorpion tattooed to her skull whose last True Love pulled a gun on her and then fled with her life savings. I was pissed at her too, because she had publicized the falsehood that I was one of her "clients" in a little write-up she got on the widely read gossip page of the New York *News-Journal*. Now that I was a semirespectable executive, I did not appreciate this kind of publicity.

Sally's beliefs were certifiably wacko and I hadn't yet figured out how to tell her this, because if you challenged her delusions she had a breakdown.

"E-Yowh E-Yowh E-YOWH," my cat, Louise Bryant, said when I opened the door. Not to anthropomorphize too much, but I believe, loosely translated, this meant, "Where the hell have you been? Don't ever leave me with the bald chick again."

She then walked to her food dish, where I noticed a mealy mixture of grains, egg, and vegetables, Sally's special blend, which she used to feed her late cat, Pie. Before I did anything else, I fed Louise the one meal she liked, cat food sautéed in oyster sauce with bok choy. As near as I can figure, she acquired a taste for this in her youth, when she was a street cat in Chinatown.

There was too much mail to go through, so I left it and checked my answering machine, which had been turned off. Louise had lately taken to sleeping on it. Sometimes her butt hit the personal-memo button, which meant either I'd hear two minutes of purring when I called in for my messages, or she'd turn it off completely. I turned it back on, called the cab company, and told them to come pick up their cab and bring spare keys, because I'd locked the one set in the glove compartment for safety. The guy on the other end had a pretty strong accent, and I was only guessing that he understood me.

For many hours, I had been spared a glimpse of myself larger than that in a rearview mirror, so it was quite a shock when I went into the bedroom and saw myself full-length. My hair was totally out of control and there wasn't a damn thing I could do with it. Lately, I'd been too busy to have my hair relaxed, and I hadn't seen much need, since I hadn't been on the air as a reporter in several months.

Bad choice. The unseasonable humidity had brought out my thick red hair's most pronounced corkscrew quality and puffed it up into a frizzy demi-'fro. I put on my costume, a black velvet dress, long black gloves, and a black scarf with a stuffed toy bat sewn on to it, so it looked like it was biting my neck. A healthy layer of waterproof white pancake, black eyeliner, and black lipstick, and I'd be all set to go out as a freshly undead person. My hair made me look like vampire Orphan Annie on steroids.

Next, I needed some weaponry for the night. I see weapons everywhere, and I have a theory about this. See, my father was a safety nut, obsessed with locating and then neutralizing the hidden menace in things. He taught me how to find the hidden menace, but he died when I was ten, before he had a chance to teach me how to thwart it. So I can usually look at something, see the menace, and though I don't know how to neutralize it, am pretty good at figuring a way to use it to defend myself. People laugh at me, but I'm a girl, a woman, whatever, alone in a big city, and—go figure—not everyone is well disposed towards me, so I feel better having this kind of knowledge.

I hadn't added any new weapons to the armory aside from upgrading to a new, improved industrial hot-glue gun, with three settings, spray, stream, and splatter, and with a rechargeable battery pack so I could go mobile with it. It weighed a ton. Normally, I don't mind, because years in NYC have made me a master schlepper. My Aunt Maureen carries a huge, heavy Bible around with her so she is always aware that God is with her. I carry a big glue gun, because I'm not always so sure about God.

But I was far too tired to schlep anything bulky or heavy like a glue gun. My Epilady hair-removal gadget was long gone and my pepper spray was empty. Screw it, I thought. I didn't need to be so paranoid tonight. For a change, I had planned a fairly sedate Girls' Night Out, on account of my young intern Kathy's coming along.

When I got back to the living room, Louise Bryant was mewling in an otherworldly way. Suddenly, she bolted off her spot and tore around the apartment, howling and jumping from the sofa to the top of a bookshelf, while I followed behind her, catching the books and things she knocked off, including a Mecca snow globe that belongs to Mike. It is not that easy to obtain a snow globe from Mecca, as you can well imagine, and this was one of Mike's treasured possessions, a gift from a young guide who had taken him through Afghanistan a few times when Mike was covering the war there as a cameraman. Thanks to a couple of like-minded young Muslim pals of his, Mike had an astounding collection of cheesy Mecca souvenirs, which he kept at my place. Above my bed, he'd hung a large painting of Mecca on black velvet.

At the window, Louise rolled around, contorting her body, still mewling as if she were in heat. A pet shrink who examined her determined that, even though Louise Bryant was elderly and had been spayed, there was still something in her head sending a Seek Sperm message. It had been jarred awake in her, he figured, by the death of Sally's cat, Pie. Since then, some wild thing had been calling her out into the night.

It's a big mean city out there, and she is an old cat with a lucrative career, so I hated to let her out. But she'd come from the streets, seemed to know her way around, and always made it home by morning. After replacing the books and the snow globe, I opened the window and carefully moved the planters full of poison ivy, which I grow to welcome unwanted visitors. Louise's gray form darted out, the filmy curtains billowing in her wake. In a flash, she was down the fire escape and out on the street, where she stopped and looked both ways. She stuck her nose up, caught some appealing scent from the east, and headed that way without hesitation.

After the day I'd had, the loudest voice in my head was telling me to take a pass on the night, make my apologies, and stay in with my entertainment system, a tasty TV dinner, and whatever was left in the Zubrowska vodka bottle in my freezer. I toyed with this idea for a while. All I had to do was call and leave a few messages on a few answering machines, and I was off the hook.

But the massive inconvenience was outweighed by my moral obligation. Not only had I invited along my intern, Kathy Loblaws, to make up for my recent neglect of her, but my other friends had lots of problems and needed my company and support. I figured I'd kill a bunch of birds with one big boulder.

I was definitely feeling a smoky, come-hither vibe from my big comfy bed. The way I saw it, I could do my mandatory friendship-and-mentoring stuff in three, four hours tops, and be in my bed by eleven.

❖ 2 ❖

"SERVE GOD TONIGHT, not the devil," screeched a guy with a plastic bloody fetus on a chain around his neck, as I stood under the giant Eight O'Clock Bean Coffee cup in Times Square, crossroads of the cosmos, waiting for Kathy the intern, who was uncharacteristically late. The nutballs were out in force tonight. It was kind of hard to tell who was in Halloween costume and who was just looney toons. After apprising me of my mission to fight the Evil One, the fetus guy pointed his finger at me, shook it angrily, and then stomped off to do the same thing to a woman clutching her purse tightly to her abdomen and a man clutching her tightly to him.

My location made me easy prey for every free-floating prophet with Mr. Microphone and a sandwich board. *"Ya na goverim Engleski,"* I said to each comer who wanted to save my soul. It's the only sentence I know in Serbo-Croatian, but it's a mighty handy one.

By seven-twenty, it was seriously dark and the big bright lights were on all over Times Square. The giant Coke bottle popped its cap and a big straw came out at regular intervals. Neon blinked, sirens whined, horns honked, some guy drummed on an overturned plastic bucket, the preachers and firebrands screamed from their soapboxes. The whole city smelled like the inside of a bus station. It was giving me a headache.

Where was Kathy the intern? I wasn't sure what costume she was wearing, but I was easily recognizable. Hard to miss a tall, undead woman with rusty Brillo Pad hair, even in Times Square.

The reason I had arranged with Kathy to meet here before going to Hojo's was so I could brief her a little more, tell her not to mention NBC, rival comedian Noriko Mori, or sumo wrestling to Tamayo Scheinman. Claire Thibodeaux was anchoring tonight, and would be meeting up with us later, so I had plenty of time to tell Kathy not to mention Jess, Washington, or the British embassy to Claire. Since Sally wasn't coming, I didn't have to tell Kathy not to bring up dead pets, bad boyfriends, or medical experiments. Maybe I worry too much, but you never know what might come up in conversation and send a sensitive and vulnerable friend into a tailspin.

By seven-thirty, after a full-frontal assault by the Jews for Jesus, one of whom answered me in Serbo-Croatian, I gave up and went to Hojo's. Kathy would figure it out. We'd picked the Hojo's restaurant in Times Square because it was central and we all liked it for different reasons, Kathy because it looked just like the one in her hometown in rural Florida, with the same decor, the same trademark orange-and-turquoise color scheme. She found it surprising to find anything in New York City that was just like back home. Tamayo and I liked it because it was such an anachronism. We liked to sit at the bar in the back, right out of 1962, and share a pitcher of anachronistic cocktails, like Rob Roys and sidecars, which were hyped on orange-and-turquoise placards on the windows.

Kathy was nowhere to be seen, but Tamayo was at the bar, with her Walkman on, dancing in her seat, singing along audibly to every third word. She was dressed like Marilyn Monroe.

"Hey, you old hooker," Tamayo said, loudly enough that people in the restaurant turned to stare at me. It would have been nice to be unobtrusive, but hard to be, looking the way I looked and with Tamayo announcing me.

We hugged. If anyone looked like a hooker, it was her. What a sight she was, Japanese face, platinum-blond wig, all five foot four of her poured into a replica of Marilyn's Happy Birthday Mr. President dress, her thin arms in sparkly white gloves. We both had a fondness for long gloves. There just aren't enough occasions in life to wear them.

"We're the only people in here in costume," I said.

"I'm not in costume."

I laughed. "Have you seen my intern Kathy?"

"No, but I don't know what she looks like."

"She knows what you look like. She'd introduce herself."

The bartender put a full pitcher of something greenish in front of Tamayo and she said, "Bartender, another glass for my dead friend."

"No thanks. I'll just have a coffee."

"No gimlet?" Tamayo said.

"I don't want to get drunk. Not even tipsy."

"But it's Halloween. . . ."

Tamayo had that special light in her eyes, the "Let's crash a debutante ball and then go throw money and roses at gay male strippers" light.

"Listen," I said. "Kathy is a nice kid, she's very serious. . . ."

"So what?"

"I just don't want anything like the dance-theater incident . . . or the bar brawl . . ."

"But we didn't start that brawl, Robin. We tried to walk away. . . ."

"I thought maybe we could try being lower-key tonight. The kid looks up to me, no shit, and it wouldn't do for her to see me drunk, swinging my bra above my head in a biker bar, for example."

"Hogs and Heifers isn't a *real* biker bar," Tamayo said.

"Nevertheless, the keyword for tonight is 'decorum.'"

"Decorum," Tamayo said, puzzled, cocking her head slightly like a dog, pretending she didn't know what it meant. "What's the intern like?"

"Young, sweet, and twenty, so she's not even old enough to drink."

"There are two kinds of women in the world, Robin, those who laugh at fart jokes, and those who don't. Does your intern laugh at fart jokes? Quality fart jokes, I mean."

"I really have no idea. Pulleeze don't get me into any trouble tonight. I'm really tired—it's been a day from hell—and I just don't know how long I'll be able to keep up with you."

Going on a tear with Tamayo requires a lot of energy, and a working woman like me needs a course of B-12 shots in preparation. The last spree I went on with her started with her one-woman show at La Mama, segued into a raucous NYU summer-school party, cruised through a couple of weird East Village bars, and ended with us getting in a bar brawl with a bunch of no-neck recently thawed cavemen from somewhere in Staten Island where toxic waste had apparently contaminated the groundwater and caused stunted brainstems and general necklessness. (There ought to be a telethon.) The cops were called, and it ended up in the gossip columns the next day. I didn't need that kind of publicity either.

Besides. I was getting a little old for barroom roughhousing.

"Here, take one of these," Tamayo said, slipping me a big fat pill.

She showed me the bottle.

"Doc Nature Seniors. Tamayo, these are vitamins for senior citizens."

"*Mega,* time-release vitamins for senior citizens. Really

powerful. You can get a serious vitamin buzz off them," Tamayo said. "They're all natural, with important amino acids and herbs and all that. They're even better than those special New York Formula vitamins."

I took it with my coffee.

"I had a rough day too," she said. "Got up at one-thirty, ate Count Chocula with chocolate milk, watched the cartoon channel for an hour, had a tarot reading with Sally, then did my Comedy Central taping," Tamayo said.

It was just a tad annoying to a grownup like me to be friends with people who could sleep until the afternoon and get away with it, especially at a time when I had been working very hard to get and stay in touch with my inner grownup. Nigh thirty, and Tamayo still lives like Pippi Longstocking, which is why she was rumored to be chapters one and seven in ANN TV psychologist and best-selling author Solange Stevenson's upcoming self-help book, *The Pippi Longstocking Complex: Girls Who Won't Grow Up*.

"How was your taping?" I asked.

"Good, did three promos, that's where I got this costume. I'm up to cohost a new show for them."

"That's great."

"Yeah, and a producer is interested in my movie."

"Man, when I left, things weren't going so good for you."

"That was then. This is now," she said, and she began to tell me about the UFO movie she was writing, inspired by one of the special reports we did on alien abductions. It was about a young woman who gets abducted by a UFO and is taken to a planet where she and other humans are farmed for bodily fluids used to make an inhalable aphrodisiac.

"There are three genders on this planet," she said. "All

three are needed to procreate, and marriages are arranged by the government. Thus the need for aphrodisiacs, inhalable, because the creatures on this planet have a combination nose and mouth. A big face hole. Did I mention they communicate not with words but with a combination of high-pitched squeaks and foul smells?"

"No, you didn't."

In Tamayo's universe, anything was possible.

"Nobody ages on the planet, because it is perched right on the edge of a black hole, which is like being on the wrong end of an inverted volcano, a volcano that sucks in instead of spewing forth."

"That would . . . suck."

"But the planet isn't sucked in, because it's caught equally between the gravitational pull of two competing black holes. It's a cosmic standoff. This gravitational hammock nestles the inhabitants at such a point that their atoms virtually stop degenerating. Time has almost stopped. The downside is, everyone weighs a lot more," she said. "Did I tell you about the free-floating inhalable fat molecules that hover about the planet, and during electrical storms the fat gets emulsified and falls to the earth in big mucusy globs, like so much frog spawn?"

"Stop! You're making me hungry."

She said something else, but I didn't hear her. I thought I saw Kathy come in with another girl. When they moved out of the shadow of the doorway, I saw they were just a couple of tourist girls, loaded down with bags from Shubert Alley gift shops.

"It's almost eight. Where is Kathy? She's *never* late," I said.

"She knows to come here, right?" Tamayo asked, a note of irritation in her voice.

"Yeah, we discussed it yesterday and I left a reminder on her voice mail this morning before I left L.A."

"Your answering machine at home was off today. Maybe she called, and when there was no answer, she used that as an excuse to flake and go out with some brooding boys instead of her boss."

"No, she wanted to go out with us."

"Of course she'd say that to you."

"She did. I told you, she looks up to me."

"Well, yeah, she looks up to you. That's why she can't be herself around you. She wants to impress you. What fun is that?"

For all of a week, I'd been Tamayo's boss. She just wouldn't take my being her boss seriously—she literally laughed out loud when I gave her orders—and when it became clear we could be friends or boss-employee but not both, she decided that she should devote herself to comedy. A half-hour before I was told to fire her for yet another smoking infraction, she quit.

I was ready to go back out to the giant coffee cup when Tamayo sighed deeply and said, "Hand me your phone. What's her number?"

She dialed and got Kathy's answering machine. "Kathy, this is Tamayo, Robin's friend. We are at Hojo's and heading down soon to the parade. Then we're going to get you roaring drunk and we're going to rumble with some sailors." Tamayo winked at me. "Call us at—" and she left my cell-phone number.

"We're covered now," she said.

"I have such a bad feeling . . ." I said.

"You worry too much," Tamayo said, and because I didn't have enough to worry about already, she tried to distract me with talk of our friend Claire's problems. Claire had recently broken up with a rising-star congressman, which had made her uncharacteristically hysterical, and shopaholic. The latest news was that a thinly disguised version of Claire was also in Solange Stevenson's book and Claire was not thrilled about it. (Reportedly and surprisingly, I was not in her book.) As a comic, Tamayo had to be childlike. Union rules. So she was proud to be the standard-bearer for Pippi. But Claire was a high-profile reporter who, of late, had worried about her reputation.

But between the two, Kathy and Claire, I was more worried about Kathy. For some reason, I thought everything would turn out wonderfully in Claire's life. I called home. There was one new message, from Mike, saying he'd definitely be in town for the weekend and hoped we could get together.

I called my voice mail at work and heard: "Robin, this is Kathy." Kathy was speaking in a loud whisper, sounding like she was trying not to giggle. "I know I'm supposed to meet you, but I'm in this man's closet and, don't laugh, his wife just came in and . . . Oh, gotta go!"

The machine beeped and I heard: "October 31, 7:54 P.M."—the time the message was left by Kathy.

I hung up and said, "She's stuck in a married man's closet."

"I told you she wasn't as sweet as you thought," Tamayo said.

"Why did she call my voice mail instead of my cell phone, or my home number?"

"She's in a closet, which is probably dark; she couldn't read her address book; so she called a number she knew by heart."

"Who is this married man?"

"None of our business," Tamayo said. "She's your intern, not your daughter. It's a mistake to get too involved in interns' personal lives. As soon as the husband gets the wife out of there, Kathy can make her escape."

"But a married man . . ." I said. True, Kathy didn't sound too worried on the phone. Still, I couldn't help thinking of her, sitting huddled in some dark closet. What if she had to pee while she was in the closet? Or sneeze? Kathy was good at being quiet, though. She sneezed like a mouse, with tiny "tu" sneezes.

I'd been there—in a married man's closet, I mean. Just after I moved to New York to go to NYU, my history prof invited me to stop by his place to discuss my grade—he gave me 60 percent for a paper and I felt I deserved *at least* a 90 percent. I was so naïve that I very innocently got talked into the bedroom, which he called his "study." Long story short, his wife came home early, because they were trying to have a baby and her temperature was right. So, while I was there, she pulled him into bed and they had sex. I was very likely present for the conception of their first kid.

"If you ever run into that kid you'll have to tell her you knew her *way* back when," Tamayo said after I told her this.

"The point is, there could be an innocent explanation for Kathy being in that closet."

Tamayo poured herself another gimlet and said, "I dunno. Sounds to me like Kathy's involved in some hanky-panky that you can't see through your illusions about her."

Granted, maybe I did have a few illusions about Kathy, a petite brunette with curls, big green eyes, an expressive face, and an enthusiasm just shy of religious ecstasy. When I imagined Kathy the intern landing in New York, I imagined her as one of those black-and-white movie heroines from the 1930s and '40s, the spunky, young, virginal, wide-eyed girl clutching her suitcase with one gloved hand and holding her beribboned hat on her head with the other.

Kathy wasn't quite that, but she sure looked like the 1990s version. No tattoos, no unusual piercings, she dressed in demure, serviceable prep clothes, good sweaters, comfortable shoes. A nice kid, hardworking, and her mother loved her. Just before she arrived, I received a secret letter from Mother Loblaws, asking me to keep an eye out for her "precious first baby."

"Kathy is a very trusting, open person so naturally I worry about someone taking advantage of her," she wrote.

She *was* very open and trusting. That's one of the things I liked about her, that freshness that had her on speaking terms with everyone from Tom, the panhandler who hung outside our building, to George Dunbar, president of the network, or, as Kathy knew them, Mr. Tom and Mr. George. That said a lot about her, I thought, the way she could be both formal with the "Mr."s and casual with the first names. The Kathy I knew had an easy yet proper friendliness to her—more proper than easy, I hoped.

As you can imagine, the letter from Kathy's mom motivated my good intentions. I started off gangbusters, helping Kathy find an affordable summer sublet and a roommate, introducing her to some of the classy, cultural stuff in New York, and taking her to a couple of editorial meetings. But then I got wrapped up in work and in solving the problems of my insane girlfriends, and instead of paying attention to Kathy I gave her a lot of busywork and sent her out in the field with the crew to shoot stock shots. Eventually she found some kind of social life outside of work, and I kinda forgot about her.

We were about to pay the bartender and head downtown to the Halloween Parade when my phone rang. It was Donna, Kathy's roommate, returning my call.

"Where's Kathy?" I said.

"She had to go meet an old friend of yours about a story on your behalf, because you were going to be late getting in from the West Coast," Donna said.

"An old friend of mine?"

"That was the message she left on our answering machine."

"Which old friend?"

"I don't know."

"The last message I got from her wasn't about that. What else did she say? What kind of story?"

"A murder story."

"A murder story? Do you know where she was supposed to meet this old friend?"

"Some Irish bar. Paddy Fitzgerald's. Does that sound right? On Seventh in the 50s."

"Yeah. I know the place. Did she say when?"

"After work."

"Donna, was Kathy involved with a man that you know of?"

"Kathy??? I don't think so. She never mentioned one."

"Did she say anything else in her message?"

"Just something about how she was going to do it, she was going to take the initiative on a story."

After I hung up, Tamayo said, "She went to meet some old friend of yours?"

"Yeah. I wonder who? It's supposedly about a murder. I hope it's not some nutty fan, although I don't have too many of those since I went off the air." My most fervently misguided fan, Elroy, was currently in a prison psych ward on heavy medication, and the rest had transferred their affections to other television personalities.

"Maybe it's some cranky ex-boyfriend of yours playing a joke," Tamayo said. "Someone who knows about you and your unhealthy interest in murder."

An ex-boyfriend. A terrible shiver went through me at those words.

Professor Balsam still taught at NYU and from what I heard he still had a thing for young coeds. But I was far too old for him now, so he wouldn't have contacted me in the first place. Howard Gollis, a dark renaissance-man comic-writer type, wasn't in town, wasn't married, and in any event had decided that I no longer existed on his planet. Most of my other ex-boyfriends were more or less happily paired off and/or not the cheating kind. God, I hoped it wasn't Chuck Turner, my back-home ex-boyfriend, in New York with his wife. Him I could easily see sneaking in a liaison while his wife was at Bloomie's spending all his money.

My intern had gone out to meet an old friend of mine about a murder and ended up in a married man's closet. Naturally, this concerned me.

☒ 3 ☒

THAT ONE WORD, "initiative," stuck in my head after I talked to Donna. Evidently, Kathy had absorbed a little from me. Just after she arrived, I took her to Buddy's, an old-timey bar where one of my mentors, Bob McGravy, used to take me when I was a sweet young thing, and I'd given her a whole lot of egotistical hot air about How I Made It in Television News, leaving out the less flattering bits about how I almost blew my career a dozen or so times, and concentrating on the more heroic side of the tale, how I'd taken risks to get this story or that story, etc., etc. If she wanted to get ahead, I practically bellowed, she had to take the *initiative,* take risks, follow her instincts. At that time, I was still being conscientious about mentoring.

The trouble is, I'd overlooked her more practical education in my rush to impress her. Damn, I meant to work on her street smarts but never quite got around to it. She hadn't yet learned all the gimmicks and artifices that can get you through stock situations in New York, like muggers trying to distract you, ex-convicts or married investment bankers trying to pick you up. She had only a little artifice, and a little artifice is worse than none or a lot in this town. It's like the producer guy says about Holly Golightly in *Breakfast at Tiffany's,* that she's a phony, but a real phony. In New York, be real or be a real phony and you can usually get along fine.

On the walk over, Tamayo talked about her movie, oblivious to the fact that I wasn't listening to her. I called Claire at ANN and left a message asking her to check my computerized phone log, see where Kathy had called me from, and call me back.

"I hope we're not here long," Tamayo said, peeking in the windows of Paddy Fitzgerald's. "An Irish bar in New York with lace curtains? Hmmm. And everyone in there is wearing a suit."

Tamayo was not enthusiastic about going to Paddy Fitzgerald's, but the place was so noisy when I'd called that I couldn't find out anything over the phone.

"What if she was lured here by some serial killer, you know, the kind who writes letters to the news media?" I said as we went in.

It had been so long since I'd been in the old Paddy Fitzgerald's, I couldn't tell if it had changed much or not, aside from having a different address from the one I'd been to. It used to be in the old Abbey Victoria Hotel, where I stayed during my first visit to New York City.

It seemed to me it used to be more Irish and convivial, more beery-smelling and less clean, that people used to stand around the piano singing. Now it was upscale. There were lots of suits and a couple of tourists. We were the only people in costume.

The bartenders directed me to the manager, who said he'd talk to us as soon as he finished seating a couple of large parties. We sat down at a recently vacated table by a window, away from the crush of hollering people at the bar.

A trim older man in a black Maxwell Smart suit and narrow tie soon came over, sat down, and told us that he remembered Kathy largely because of the murder mystery. About a week earlier, a woman had called up and asked if the bar would participate in a murder mystery for charity. In gratitude, a donation would be made in the bar's name to a children's charity called Help for Kids, which he had

checked out with New York State. It was a legitimate charity run by some woman named Anne Winston.

"Marty, can you come here?" a waiter called to the manager.

"Excuse me," he said. "I'll be right back."

"It's some kind of publicity stunt," Tamayo said. "Now
you can stop worrying."

"It still doesn't explain how she ended up in a married
man's closet instead of under the giant coffee cup."

"What could happen to her while the wife is there? And
at least you know she wasn't abducted by a serial killer or
a space alien."

When I opened my mouth to express my concern again,
Tamayo said, "Remember when I went out to field-
produce the story on the guy who was suing to get his
donated kidney back from his alcoholic brother, who was
ruining the organ with drinking . . ."

"I remember."

". . . and when the crew showed up to meet me I wasn't
there because I was out late the night before doing stand-
up and I fell asleep on the subway and rode it all the way
out to Far Rockaway. I couldn't call you because I didn't
have a cell phone and I couldn't find a phone that
worked. . . ."

Yeah, and I'd gone out to the kidney guy's place and
demanded to see my producer Tamayo, because I was convinced he'd made his whole story up in order to abduct
young female journalists. Got completely hysterical, practically tore his place apart. This was, I hasten to add, perfectly justifiable, since it came not long after I'd been
kidnapped, and not long after I took over the Special Reports unit and became responsible for other human beings.

The next day Tamayo gave me an apology card inside
which she had written: "Did you know that doctors in

France once prescribed something called Dr. Raspail's vaginal camphor cream for female hysteria?"

No, I didn't know. And where can I get some?

"Remember the time I got kidnapped?" I countered, dialing the Help for Kids number. I got another answering machine with what sounded like a computerized voice. After explaining the missing-intern situation, I left my number.

The manager came back and hurriedly explained, "Today, a FedEx arrived containing a square white envelope and a receipt for a large donation to Hale House. The square envelope was to be given to the customer who came up to the bar and answered a skill-testing question. The young woman with the curly brown hair . . ."

"Kathy."

"She got the answer right, so I gave her the envelope."

"What was the question?" I asked.

"Where is it? . . . Who won the Arne Olsen Scholarship in 1978?" he said.

"I won that scholarship," I explained to Tamayo.

"And Kathy knew that?"

"I may have mentioned it once or twice." Plus, I had the certificate on my office wall and it was in my ANN bio.

"She, Kathy, was surprised to hear it was a murder mystery, but she laughed when I told her," the manager said.

"So it's some publicity thing, to get media people to follow clues to something," I said. In the competition to get media attention in New York City, PR people often sent enticing things designed to grab attention, and they often addressed you in their letters as if you were old friends. They had evidently tailor-made this gimmick to flatter me, I told Tamayo, and probably there were other media people at other places picking up clues after answering skill-testing questions about their own modest accomplishments.

"What time was she here?"

"That was, oh, two, three hours ago. I hadn't been here long, a half-hour maybe, and I start work at five. Can't be more specific than that. It's been crazy tonight."

"Did she talk to anyone else? A man?"

"Not that I saw."

"Did she leave with someone?"

"No, I definitely saw her leave alone."

"Did she say anything else?" I said.

"She asked where Chez Biftek was. I looked it up in the book for her."

When he went to look up the address for us, Tamayo said, "I know nothing bad is going to happen to Kathy, because my horoscope promised a fabulous night. Sally has been right on the money about everything this week. You know, I could use this in my UFO movie I'm writing—a young woman is hiding in a married man's closet when suddenly she gets beamed up to a space ship. . . ." Then she said nothing. She had fugued, going to whatever planet she came from, and I fugued too, looking out the window at the spot where the Abbey Victoria used to be.

Nineteen seventy-nine. Seemed like such a long time ago. I missed the old Abbey, a grand old middle-class hotel in midtown Manhattan, along with the Taft, the Wellington, and a handful of others. The revolving doors at the entrance led to a dozen marble steps and up into a large marble lobby with chandeliers and bellmen in red uniforms and bellboy caps. The clerk behind the desk wore a bow tie. The Broadway-tour ticket agent chomped on a cigar in a dark, cluttered cubbyhole of an office with fading posters of Lunt and Fontanne and Helen Hayes on the walls. All the fixtures, from the old-fashioned switchboard to the

brass-and-glass letter chutes between the elevators on every
floor, were from another era. If it weren't for the guests,
in their decidedly 1970s clothes (there was a big disco convention in town), I would have thought I'd just stepped
into another decade.

The hotel was struggling to survive and it was, I now
realized, kind of down in the mouth, a bit seedy and frayed
at the edges—our window looked out into a sooty brick
windshaft—though it seemed very big-city and glamorous
to me back then. It must have been a bear to maintain that
huge hotel, especially for the largely aged staff. I remembered the old, shrunken bellman who took me and my
friend Julie up to our room. Imagine Conan O'Brien if you
freeze-dried him. He wheezed dramatically, stopping every
ten feet or so to sit atop our bags and catch his breath.
When we offered to carry our own bags, he refused to allow
it. We felt so guilty we tipped him $10 each, a lot of money
to us.

After I moved to New York, I used to get a kick out of
going down there and standing in the lobby, reliving my
first exciting days in New York City. Then they tore it
down to put up a big square box of an office building.

I said to Tamayo, "You know, this is the first New York
bar I went into during my first trip to New York."

"This place?"

"Yeah. I came here with my friend Julie and we met two
rich guys who were just *so* nice to us. Well, one of them
was, George. He *dazzled* us with New York. God, and we
just abused him and his friend Billy, told them a bunch of
whoppers."

Funny, that used to be a pleasant memory, but now I
felt lousy and guilty about lying to those guys.

"What did you tell them?"

"That my friend Julie and I were half-sisters and iron-works heiresses. We talked about the horsey boarding school we'd attended, country-club balls, and—oh, man— I think we may even have told a few amusing stories about our loyal and lovable old servants."

"Ironworks?"

"I come from iron country."

The manager came back with the address of Chez Biftek. Tamayo wanted me to call. But you get more information face to face, and it was another short walk over to 47th Street and Eighth Avenue.

The name was different, so I didn't realize until we got there, but I'd been to Chez Biftek before too, or, rather, another restaurant just off Restaurant Row in the same narrow little townhouse with a red awning and red shut-tered windows.

"Cosmic that you were at both these places," Tamayo said.

"Not cosmic, just an amazing coincidence," I replied, though I got a weird chill when I went down the stairs and opened the wooden door. It was a pretty amazing coinci-dence, because I'd been here right after being at Paddy Fitzgerald's the first time.

When it was Table Bas, I'd been terribly impressed by the cosmopolitan flavor of it, a real French restaurant in New York. But, boy, had it changed. Now it was one of those places that paid the tour companies to herd tourists in beneath Paris travel posters and made the poor tourists eat rubbery snails and tough cuts of meat smothered in sauce, prepared by Guatemalans and brought to them by Polish or Russian waiters with fake French accents.

In keeping with the spirit of the night, the maître d' and

all the waiters were dressed like harlequins. The maître d' called someone, and then directed us through the kitchen to the back office. There was no answer when we knocked on the manager's door, but the door was half open, so I pushed it and stepped into the room. As soon as I did, a man in harlequin costume with bloody eyes fell forward onto me, revealing the knife handle sticking out of his back.

I screamed. Tamayo screamed.

Then the dead harlequin with the knife in his back screamed.

We all screamed.

"Haaaappy Halloweeeeen," the man said, laughing.

For a moment there, I was so stunned that I couldn't feel my heart beating. I had to check my pulse to make sure I hadn't had a coronary. It wouldn't have been the first time I'd walked into an office and found a dead person, an experience I wasn't keen on reliving.

"You scared the . . . What was that about?"

The man was laughing his ass off as he peeled off the bloody eyeballs. Tamayo thought it was pretty funny too.

"Part of the mystery," he said. "It has worked . . . both times tonight. Ha-ha-ha."

When he managed to regain his composure, he gave us the same charity-murder-mystery story. Kathy had come in and picked up an envelope after answering a skill-testing question about the year the ANN Special Reports unit won an ACE award for our series on vigilantism.

"Okay, so then you gave her the envelope and she opened it."

". . . and pulled out a photograph and a folded paper square with a note inside." He didn't see what it was, but she asked him if he could look up the address of Joy II for her.

"That was around five-forty-five-ish, thereabouts," he said.

"Did she talk to any strange men, leave with anyone?"

"I don't think so."

"Mind if I talk to the rest of the staff?"

"Go ahead."

"Thanks," I said. "No, don't get up. We'll see ourselves out."

"Happy Halloween," he said again, still laughing.

While I quizzed the staff about Kathy, Tamayo was recognized by a couple from Indiana who had seen her on television. This improved her already blithe mood considerably.

I felt a little less blithe. Chez Biftek made me uncomfortable, and not only because of Kathy, the undead harlequin, and the poor tourists forced to eat expensive bad French food prepared by illegal aliens. I felt hugely embarrassed by the memory of Table Bas. The rich guy George, I remembered aloud to Tamayo as we departed, insisted on coming here, and he ordered in French, which impressed the hell out of us. "Robin speaks French," my friend Julie had said, adding that I'd learned it while we modeled in Paris the summer before. This was another joke/lie, like the one that I was an ironworks heiress. Beyond "*Où est la discothèque?*," "*Aimez-vous les sports?*," "*Voulez-vous couchez avec moi çe soir?*," and a few other phrases I'd memorized phonetically before a four-day school trip to Montreal, I spoke NO French back then.

Encouraged, George spilled off a waterfall of French, and his friend Billy asked me what George was saying. I was so afraid I was going to be exposed, but George jumped in and said, "I told her she is a very pretty and very smart

young woman, and she could do well in New York." And
he winked at me.

Oh God, I realized now, he must have known I was
faking the French. I was so naïve, I thought I'd gotten away
with it. Now I was experiencing retroactive embarrassment.
But even if they didn't buy the French part, I thought,
maybe they bought the rest of it. People believe what they
want to believe. Just ask the woman in Tulsa who had sex
with a video-store owner because he told her he was an
extraterrestrial who'd adopted human form. According to
the video-store owner, she wasn't the only woman who'd
fallen for it, but she was the only one who admitted it.
Even scarier: the woman voted regularly.

"So now what?" Tamayo said.

"On to the next stop."

"I hope we can go downtown to the parade after that,"
Tamayo said wistfully.

She started singing the Petula Clark song "Downtown"
at the top of her lungs to me, hamming it up to the nth,
while I shook my head in a mildly amused, mildly embarrassed grownup way. Out of a dingy-looking apartment
building wedged between a deli and a closed-up gay porn
place on Eighth Avenue came a gaggle of fine-looking drag
queens, dressed to the nines—bouffant hair, false eyelashes,
and shimmering dresses in bright colors that looked like
they were made with the pelts of mythical creatures. One
of them, a black queen, was doing Marilyn too.

"Sing it, girl," he said to Tamayo, and he chimed in.
Tamayo and the black Marilyn danced ahead of the rest of
us, mirroring each other's movements like on "The Patty
Duke Show."

I wished I could be that carefree, but I couldn't quiet
my anxiety about Kathy. That dead harlequin must have
scared the shit out of her too.

Kathy didn't sound worried on the phone, Tamayo wasn't worried, there had to be a logical explanation, all this I was willing to accept. I know I have a tendency to push the panic button at times, so I was trying really hard to keep my finger off the button as we approached Joy II and I saw its giant neon naked-woman sign.

❖ 4 ❖

"This is a strange place for a charity murder mystery to benefit kids," I said. "This has to be a mistake."

"Politically incorrect at least," Tamayo said.

A strip joint set on 45th Street just off Eighth Avenue, Joy II was one of a diminishing breed. This stretch of Eighth used to be a complete sleaze strip, one nudie joint and peep-show palace after another in a sea of neon X's and flickering marquee lights, but it had been cleaned up a lot, largely through attrition. When a sleaze joint's lease ran out, it was kicked out to make room for a more "respectable" business, and the landlord got some kind of big redevelopment tax break. It was part of the Disneyfication of Times Square. I know it sounds strange, Disney and Times Square, but if they can make Quasimodo "cuddly," maybe they could clean up Times Square. Personally, I prefer the monstrous beauty of Lon Chaney's Quasimodo, but to each his own.

Behind the ticket window was a woman, about sixty, with bright-red lips and silver hair piled on her head and held in place with a mesh of hairspray. Some large drops of hairspray had hardened like tree sap and were glistening in the marquee lights.

"Rochelle, it's Goldie. I got my stitches out yesterday," she was saying to someone on the telephone. In her bulletproof glass capsule, her voice sounded like it was coming from Apollo 13.

"Excuse me," I said.

She ignored me. "Maybe you should see a doctor. What color is your sputum?"

"Excuse me . . ." I said, this time more urgently.

She put her hand over the phone. "What?!?"

"Can I ask you some questions? It's fairly important."

She sighed deeply, hugely annoyed at my intrusion, and swatted at a fly that was buzzing around her booth. "Goldenseal is good, I hear. I'll see you at dinner Sunday. Gotta go."

She hung up the phone, and looked at me hard, resentful because I'd interrupted her conversation about Rochelle's phlegm.

"What?"

"I'm looking for a girl who came here about a murder mystery. I can't find her now. . . ."

"You're too late. Someone was already here for that. Went in and spoke with the manager, then left," Goldie said. The fly landed on her hair and got stuck there. I was distracted for a moment watching it try to extricate itself from the sweat and hairspray.

"Can I speak to the manager?" I asked. "Find out where . . ."

"Admission is ten dollars a head," said Goldie.

I slapped a twenty down and shoved it through the money slot.

She pushed it back and pointed to a sign that said "No Unescorted Women."

Some people just get off on fucking with other people, and Goldie was clearly one of them. But I guess if you're nearing retirement and you're working in a ticket booth in a Times Square strip joint, your life probably hasn't worked out the way you planned and you have to find your amusement where you can. You could sort of see, through the deeply etched wrinkles, all pointing down, that she had had a hard life but could have been really pretty at one time. Probably, she wanted to be Marilyn Monroe.

"You're holdin' up the line," she said.

There was no line, but we stepped away all the same.

"I'm amazed that Kathy, coming this far, bothered to go in for the clue, even if she didn't have to ask a strange man to escort her in. God, I hope she didn't ask a strange man to escort her in. Then he abducted her and took her to his apartment. That's when his wife walked in and pulled out her revolver and . . ."

"Robin, calm down. . . ."

"Naïve or not, she is not completely aware of all the terrible things that can happen to you in a big city like New York on a night like Halloween. . . ."

"You're starting to sound like your Aunt Maureen. . . ."

Boy, did that put the fear of God in me, being compared to my Aunt Maureen. As soon as Tamayo said that, I heard the voice of my Aunt Mo in the back of my head, before I came to New York the first time, saying, "Don't go to New York! It's full of atheists and perverts just waiting for a lamb to stumble into the slaughterhouse." She was so sure I'd be set upon by white-slavers and pornographers and people who would hide drugs in my suitcase to be smuggled back to their nefarious contacts in northern Minnesota. For two months before the trip, she sent me clippings from newspapers about bad things happening to young women in New York.

On the other hand, she wasn't completely wrong about New York. At various points in my life here, I *had* been set upon by pimps and perverts and murderers.

"I should have taught Kathy how to scream her way out of a jam, or bought her that lupus book, or a glue gun . . ." I said to Tamayo.

"That woman said Kathy was just here. That means she got out of the apartment, came here, and should be calling you soon," Tamayo said.

Tamayo had cruised through life on laughter and good luck, so she tended to see things as a little rosier than I suspected they were. Tonight she was in her transcendentally confident mode, her belief that, if you keep a light heart, ultimately everything will work out as well as it possibly can in a life that ends with death.

But she had a point too. A couple of hours had elapsed between Kathy's stop at Chez Biftek and her stop here. That would account for her time in the closet. But why hadn't she called me yet?

"Did you come here that night in 1979?" Tamayo asked.

"God, no. The amazing coincidences have ended," I said, punching in Kathy's apartment phone number on my cell phone to see if she'd called Donna. Donna had gone out and turned on the answering machine. There were no new messages for me at home or at work.

Two guys came up, both with baseball caps pulled low over their eyes. Tamayo grabbed one. "Will you guys take us into this place?"

"Uh, wow! Yeah," one said, sounding like he was making his voice lower than it was naturally. "Good costumes."

As soon as we got inside, we cheerfully and unceremoniously ditched them to talk to a bouncer, who told us we wanted to speak to Candy, who was MC'ing the show in the Pussycat Room.

It took a while for my eyes to adjust to the dark. There are classy strip places in New York, male and female, if that's what you're into. This wasn't one of them, but it was far from the worst place I'd been in, and it even had some artistic pretensions. On a stage in front of a backdrop painted, badly, to look like a jungle, several extremely big-breasted "dancers" were taking off their faux animal skins in front of a room of men in baseball caps. I recognized the music, it was Yma Sumac singing some 1940s jungle-

movie song—Yma's operatic voice against the background
of thumping drums and deep-voiced chanting men. It's
very primal stuff, and made me think of my occasional
boyfriend Eric, because he loved Yma Sumac and liked to
play her CDs during sex. Great take-me-now-wild-man
kind of music, and this display was ruining the memory
for me. The place smelled of I don't know what. I hoped
I didn't smell this smell from now on whenever I heard
Yma Sumac.

"This is every horny little straight boy's Saturday-
matinee dream come true," I whispered.

"Yeah! Like a Tarzan movie where Jane takes her
clothes off."

"It's almost . . . Disneyesque."

"Why would any woman want breasts as big as regu-
lation basketballs? Think they knock a lot of stuff over
with those?" Tamayo asked, exaggerating slightly. Her eyes
swept the shadowy audience. "And look at all these bottle-
fed babies."

"Sssh," said a man ahead of us.

This was a different crowd from the yuppies who went
to upscale clubs like Scores on the Upper East Side and
The Platinum in the Flatiron District, or boho strip joints
like Billy's Topless A-Go-Go or Blue Angel. This was
strictly what *les snobs* call bridge-and-tunnel traffic, mama's
boys from Jersey and the outer boroughs who come in to
42nd Street looking for something very specific to their
tastes. In this instance, very big breasts.

"Are these guys jerking off?" Tamayo said, peering
around. "Oh God, they are."

"We've seen guys jerk off before. Don't act so impressed."

"It never fails to impress me, though," Tamayo said.

"I can't watch," I said, and turned away. "That woman in the middle? An accident waiting to happen."

All that hardened silicone was dangerous, and I knew it was silicone, because they were just too big and round to stand up that way on their own. I was afraid she'd swing 'em a bit too briskly, and the weight would throw her into the audience and injure some poor sap. I was fairly certain she could kill a man with those enormous tatas.

My phone rang, drawing several ssssh's, so I went back through the heavy black curtains to stand in the foyer until the show was over.

"Robin? Claire. Kathy called you from 555-0318," she said very quickly. She was between shows and hadn't much time.

That was the Help for Kids number.

"Next break you get, can you check out this charity for me? Where is it, who is involved. I'll explain later."

"Okay. I'll call youse guys soon," she said, and hung up.

That was when I saw the word "Malabar" inlaid in the foyer's tile ceiling. Of course. This used to be the Malabar Theater, and then later the Malabar Disco. After we'd gone to the French restaurant that night in 1979, we'd all come here. We danced and drank with Billy and George. We danced and drank with a Saudi prince and a Finnish mogul. Julie told the mogul I spoke Finnish. Lucky for me the music was so loud I was able to pretend I didn't hear her or him. I should have just told him she was lying, but I was afraid, after all the lies we'd told that night, if I confessed one I might just keep going and confess them all. It was a burden keeping up that multilingual-heiress persona.

Three different places from that night in New York. Celestine Prophecy notwithstanding, I was beginning to think this was no cosmic coincidence.

The curtains parted and a stream of men in lowered baseball caps filed out, followed by a bouncer, followed by Tamayo and an extremely buxom, fully dressed brunette in her thirties or forties.

"I'm Candy," she said. "You wanna talk? Come with me."

Tamayo went outside to smoke while Candy and I went into her grotesquely girly office, a bright-pink room with lots of flowers, heart-shaped things, and posters of "Candy Apples" in her heyday as a stripper.

"If you do a story, I hope you'll do a positive story about the charity work we do. And that we do a whole theatrical production here, costumes, sets, music. . . . It's, whaddya call it, like burlesque, Gypsy Rose Lee. We're classy. We're completely out of the live-sex business, have been for almost a year."

"Uh, okay," I said, as I tried to figure out the decor. She had kind of a Barbara Cartland–meets–Al Goldstein thing going in here. (Barb and Al, that's a live-sex show I'd pay money to see, but only on an empty stomach.)

"A woman came by not long ago to pick up an envelope?"

"Yeah, and it was over a half hour ago, before the eight-thirty show."

"Over a half hour ago?" Then she certainly should have called me by now. "Was she alone?"

"As far as I knew. Someone must have escorted her in. . . ."

"She left alone—"

Candy cut me off. "Alone and in a big hurry," she said.

"Did she open the envelope here? Do you know where . . ."

"No."

"How did you get mixed up in this, who . . ."

"Why not? It's for charity, for kids! We do a lot for charity. We like kids. Lots of us here have kids. We're a woman-owned business. We pay our taxes. We vote," she said, a *tad* defensively. As this unsolicited recitation of her good-citizen credentials showed, she was feeling the Disneyfication pressure.

"What do you know about Help for—"

"I checked them out with New York State. It's a legit nonprofit corporation, okay? I got a call a while back asking if we'd take part. Then I got a FedEx today with an envelope and a receipt for a donation to charity."

"What was the skill-testing question?"

"The what?"

"Wasn't there a skill-testing question attached to the envelope?"

"I didn't see one," she said, leaning over to dig through her trash. When she did, she knocked a pencil cup off her desk with her breasts.

She found a FedEx envelope and handed it to me. "Help for Kids," it said in the "From" space, and gave a P.O. box. Inside, stuck in the crease, was a slip of paper with a paper clip attached.

"Who broke the dress code at Hummer High school in 1975?" it said, referring to a time when we fought passionately for the right to wear polyester shirts, gold chains, blue eye shadow, and platform shoes.

On the other side of the paper, it said, "Answer: Lucky Jake." Lucky Jake was me, or, rather, the male pseudonym under which I wrote humor for the school newspaper (since it had become clear to me that boys didn't seem to go for the funny girls, and I liked boys a lot). I didn't break the code alone, though my reports on the goofy clothes the teachers wore when they were our age and what teachers and parents thought about it then helped galvanize the dress-code liberals, and we won the right to wear really ugly clothes if we so chose.

These charity people had gone to extraordinary lengths to kiss my ass.

"Did the woman who picked up the envelope open it?"

"Not here," Candy said.

Now I sized her up. She didn't look like the kind of woman who would give an envelope to someone without first checking what was inside it.

"Did you happen to see what was in the envelope?"

She didn't answer right away, and I said, "Look, my intern, this twenty-year-old girl from rural Florida, she's been following these clues, and now I've lost her. It's really important to me that I find her."

Candy located a small key on the crowded key ring, opened her top desk drawer, and pulled out a sheet of paper.

"I can't be too careful," she said. "I have enemies. I didn't want anyone to set me up."

She handed me two sheets of paper. The first was a photocopy of a typed note that read:

Robin, thanks for coming this far. It's for a good cause. The newspaper clipping will explain some of it, and you'll understand the rest later. Backslash Cafe.

The second sheet was a handwritten note dated August 7, 1979, which said, "Where the Blue Moon burned down." It was signed "Putli Bai." The Blue Moon was a supper club in my hometown, and Putli Bai an alias I was familiar with.

Holy shit, I thought.

The first photocopy had what looked like creases copied into the paper. I asked Candy about it and she said, "It was all folded up, like one of those thing kids used to have. Whaddya call 'em? Cootie catchers."

Even if I hadn't known about the cootie catcher, or seen the trademark signature or the skill-testing question, I would have known by the handwriting on the second sheet that this was from Julie Goomey. God, it was strange to see Julie Goomey's handwriting again, which hadn't improved much over the years, with its t-crossing flourishes and extra-loopy loops that shifted whimsically from left to right as if blown back and forth by the wind.

Looking at it brought back the memory of a thousand notes covertly exchanged during classes. One time in eighth grade, Julie got me out of my dreaded sewing class by saying she had a note from the principal. Thank God Mrs. Hobbins, the sewing teacher, didn't read the note, which said, in Julie's unprincipallike blue scratch, "Tell Robin Hudson to get her ass down to the office before I kick it to China. Signed, the Principle." Of course she had misspelled "principal."

"Where's the clipping?" I asked.

"There was none," Candy said.

No clipping—that was a classic Julie-esque stroke. Something she often did when someone didn't write her back promptly was send an empty envelope to pique the person's curiosity—or worse.

One time she sent me a letter from Ohio, where she was looking after a sick relative, with the last page of a three-page letter that began midsentence with, "to get her letter and hear some of the news from Ferrous. I hope you don't take what she said about you the wrong way. You know how she is and have to consider the source." I was of course so frantic to find out who had said what about me and why I might be offended that I picked up the phone and called her, running up a $30 long-distance bill. Actually, I'd always kind of resented that particular tactic of hers, but Julie never knew that, so she probably thought the clipping was just a cute variation on it.

Then there was the time, in tenth grade, when I found a typed love letter signed "Doug Gribetz," this boy I was *mad* for, in my locker, asking me to talk to him and let him know if I felt the same way about him as he felt about me. When I told Julie about it, she admitted that she had written the note. Come to think of it, I had always resented that little joke too, though I was grateful Julie told me before I went to Doug and completely embarrassed myself.

Candy knew no more than what she'd told me, or so she said. After thanking her, I handed her my card and said, "If anyone else comes by, or you remember something else, call me."

"Sure."

Now I could relax. Obviously, this was all an elaborate stunt of Julie's, and Kathy was in on it, if not from the beginning, then certainly by now. There'd probably be a big celebration at the end, just like the time Julie set up a series of clues that led me to my surprise sixteenth-birthday party. Once I finished throttling Julie for making me worry so damn much, we'd have a hearty laugh and reminisce about the good old days. Many was the story I told Kathy about the pranks my friends played at ANN. She knew I had a good appreciation for a quality prank. Still, it surprised me that Kathy, sweet Kathy, could be so inconsiderate, scaring me like this.

But if she'd hooked up with Julie . . . well, Julie could be very persuasive. Just ask our childhood torturer, Mary MacCosham, whom Julie once sent to Minneapolis on a fake modeling audition at a nonexistent address.

Better yet, ask the rival Valhalla High football and pep

squads, who, with the help of our high-school drama club and some very official-looking party posters, were lured to a "beer party" and ended up fifty miles out of town at a tent revival while we stole their mascot, the Iron Maiden, whom we thoroughly degraded.

Julie and I had had some great Girls' Nights Out, legendary. It kinda felt like old times, having her play a part in this one.

✵ 5 ✵

TAMAYO WAS OUT on the street smoking. A man either not in costume, or in costume as a seedy Times Square lowlife, was leaning on the wall next to her, trying to pick her up under a faded sign promising "Air Conditioned Comfort," painted on the brick wall of the old Malabar building.

"Hey, Bob," Tamayo said to me, in her deepest, most masculine voice, which she was able to pull off somewhat better than the lonely little men inside Joy II. Our friend Sally claimed this was due to Tamayo's being someone called Ruby Helder, girl tenor, in her last life.

"Aw, c'mon, you're not really men," the guy said to me. "Are you?"

"We're cops on undercover duty. No time for idle chitchat now," I said, using my tough sailor voice and quickly flashing my NYPD press pass. "There's a perp on 42nd. . . ."

The guy looked like he wasn't sure, and these days you can't be too sure, especially with a half-Asian in a blond wig and a tight sequined dress on Halloween. Then he said, "Sorry," walking away a few steps casually before beating a retreat.

"You have to stop doing that," I said. "One of these days we'll get gay-bashed by one of these freaks."

"There's something about me that attracts these guys. I'm giving off a pheromone," Tamayo said.

"That, or the fact that you're gigged up as Marilyn Monroe and standing outside a strip joint."

"I dunno. I've been hit on by a lot of guys in ratty brown shoes lately. So what did Candy say?"

After I filled her in, she said, "So, if this is a stunt, we don't have to worry anymore, right? We can go down to Sam Chinita and grab a quick bite, then see some of the parade on our way downtown," Tamayo said.

"A quick bite, sure. I'm starving. That vitamin hasn't kicked in yet."

"This Julie was a good friend of yours?" Tamayo asked.

"My best friend for years since just after she moved to Ferrous in fifth grade until the summer before I moved to New York. Haven't seen her since 1979. We had a big falling out."

"But why a murder mystery?"

"When we were kids, we used to do these mysteries," I said. "My mom started it, as a party game for my twelfth birthday. We followed clues until we solved the mystery and got to a treasure. Julie and I did this a lot for birthdays, and whenever we had a falling out and needed to make up."

"Instead of just saying you were sorry and talking it out or anything crazy like that," Tamayo said.

"Well, this way you didn't have to actually say you were sorry or admit out loud that you were in the wrong. It was also more fun."

"It is pretty funny," Tamayo said. "But you haven't talked to her in all these years, and this is the way she gets back in touch with you, inviting you along on a charity-mystery thingie? She couldn't pick up the phone and call you?" She sounded just like her Jewish grandmother on Long Island when she said that, which is just a bit jarring, hearing that voice coming out of her.

"Yeah, I thought that too. But this is Julie. And I think it must be like overdue-library-book syndrome. You leave something so long that you're embarrassed to take the book back, or pick up the phone, whatever. She was always really good at these things."

"You want to see her after all these years?" Tamayo asked.

"Yeah. She was a pistol. She'd laugh at a quality fart joke," I said, growing suddenly sentimental. "Taught me a lot, Julie Goomey. She taught me how to draw a perfect three-dimensional horse head, taught me double dutch. She taught me how to pee standing up."

"You can pee standing up?"

"Yeah. It's easy, all you need is a simple kitchen funnel, in whatever size is appropriate for you."

This is particularly handy if you're on a camp out in the woods and want to avoid brambles, bugs, or embarrassing sneaker splatter. With a little funnel manipulation, you can even write your name in the snow.

"Damn. Julie Goomey, after all these years. It'll be good to see her and catch up, give me a chance to thank her."

"For what? Teaching you how to pee standing up?"

"If it wasn't for Julie Goomey, I would never have moved to New York."

For that reason alone, I owed her. I owed her for a few other things too.

Speaking of accidents that send one's life spinning in an unexpected direction, my life would have been so different if it wasn't for Julie Goomey. In 1979, Julie Goomey and I were in Ferrous, Minnesota, going to community college part-time and working full-time, me managing a Burger King, Julie in accounting at Groddeck Motors. Every Friday night, we put on our Calvin Kleins, so tight we had to lie down on the bed to get them on, and went with our boyfriends Chuck and Lance to Ye Olde Pizza Factory, then to a movie or the roller disco, where we drank Boone's Farm strawberry wine in the parking lot because the disco was dry. I admit that I never liked disco, and even now the strains of "Stayin' Alive" bring a green tinge to my skin, but it was fashionable then, so I went along with it, secretly listening to country rock on my eight-track player while obsessing over my Rubik's Cube at home.

(Funny, but what I most remember about the period before we decided to go to New York is not Chuck, college, disco, or even the hostages in Tehran, but Rubik's Cube. I was addicted to it. It got so bad I took my Cube with me everywhere, to parties, to work, to my boyfriend Chuck's sporting events. When he looked up from the ice after scoring a game-winning goal in a pickup hockey game and saw me not watching him but clicking my Cube, he gave me a choice: him or the Cube. After that, I worked on it secretly, ducking into the john, taking it out of my purse, and giving it a few spins. I think one of the reasons I was so obsessed with it was that Julie had solved it pretty easily, whereas I was baffled. Only when my grades started to suffer did I finally drive my car over my Rubik's Cube to remove the temptation. I never picked up another one.)

By this time, Julie Goomey and I had abandoned our adolescent dreams—I had wanted to be a television reporter (which had replaced crime-fighting cowgirl) and she had wanted to be a painter (which had replaced bandit queen)—and, spurred by the illusion of True Madness, we now dreamed the same dream, to marry our boyfriends, buy nice houses in Ferrous, and raise nice kids. Except for the part about marrying my then boyfriend, that dream still sounds pretty decent to me, though for me it is no longer achievable.

Then we went to New York, and it changed everything.

When Julie first suggested going to New York for spring break in 1979, I balked. Our boyfriends had been planning since fall to go to Florida to cheat on us, and naturally I wanted to go down there too and spy on them. But Chuck got wise to my spy plan and made it clear that not only was I forbidden to set foot in Florida, but he would look unkindly on my going to any warm-weather place. I know, I know. Hard to believe that I, Robin Hudson, was ever so docile, but I was going through a powerful conformity phase, so, rather than upset him, I agreed to stay off beaches.

That's when Julie said, "Let's go to New York and shop."

The boys found this to be an inoffensive alternative. Better to have us shopping in parkas in chilly New York than dancing drunk in bikinis on a tropical beach somewhere. So, while they planned their "Daytona Drunk," as they referred to it, Julie and I planned our trip to the Big City. I was still worried about Chuck's trip to Florida, but Julie's enthusiasm for New York helped motivate me. The New York trip was the first thing to excite me since I'd given up the Cube. I went to the library and photocopied whole chapters from guidebooks, clipped out magazine articles, wrote away for all sorts of brochures.

Back in the 1970s, New York boasted three bank robberies an hour and five murders a day. Affluent Manhattan parents gave their kids "mugger's money" when they went out, so they had something to hand over in case they got held up. Clearly, Julie and I needed "street smarts." We studied up on the rules, so we wouldn't look like the complete rubes we were. Hold your purse close to you, the advice to out-of-towners went. Don't make eye contact, don't talk to strangers, don't look up at the buildings.

We followed the "rules"—for about an hour. There was so much to gawk at. I mean, if you followed those rules you could visit New York, spend a week here, and leave without really seeing any of the sights or talking to anyone. Anyway, all the trouble we took to learn those rules, and people in New York instantly knew we were from out of town. Go figure.

On our agenda were the usual tourist things, Broadway shows, the Empire State Building, shopping at Saks, Macy's, and Bloomingdale's. We also wanted to eat at an automat (like Marlo Thomas did in "That Girl"), dance at Studio 54, go to an Andy Warhol party (after reading about such things in *People* magazine), and meet exciting, cultured men who would be dazzled by us, though we would remain loyal to our undeserving and morally inferior boyfriends, at least as far as I was concerned (after reading that newsmagazine cover story about "Herpes, the New Scarlet Letter," and how it was cutting a swath through New York's singles scene).

The night we went out with George and Billy to Table Bas, the Malabar, and points south was the second night we were in New York, our first real night out, since we'd arrived late the previous evening. We were on a budget, so, instead of taking a cab when we arrived in New York, we took the JFK express subway train, only to get off at the wrong stop and get caught in a torrential rain. Unable to hail a cab, we walked, dragging our suitcases, stopping en route in a coffee shop called Two Joes to warm up and dry off a bit. I remember I had a moment of déjà vu there, which is strange, having a déjà vu in a city you've never been to before. When we finally got to the hotel, we changed into our jammies, blew-dry our hair, and ordered the cheapest things we could from room service. We were exhausted from the trip and a bit too intimidated by the city to go back out into it on our first night. While we watched a TV with terrible reception (even New York didn't have cable then), Julie Goomey marked a map with red pen, highlighting all the places we wanted to go.

I could still see her sitting on her bed, smiling so sweetly, chewing on her red pen while very conscientiously considering our route. I had a photo of that somewhere.

On our second night, after an all-day Grayline bus tour, we went down to the hotel bar, Paddy Fitzgerald's, and there met Billy and George as they were coming out of the men's room together. George grabbed Julie's arm and said, "You are the most beautiful girl I've ever seen. You look just like Marie Osmond, only better." Something like that. It was a long time ago, we drank a lot that night, and the details are kind of a blur.

This I do remember clearly: George's friend Billy wasn't very friendly at first and said, "We really should be going."

"Whaddya talkin' about? We'll have a drink with the girls," George said. "You're not going to walk out on two beautiful girls like this, are you?" He had a strong accent, I now recall. He said beautiful girls, "buhyootiful goils."

Though I was a bit leery, Julie, who had a nose for money, took note of the gold cufflinks, the Rolex watch, and the expensive suits, and cheerfully accepted his invitation.

"You're models, right?" George said.

We did not yet know that this was an already old pickup line in places like New York, and we were incredibly flattered. That's when our lies began. We sat in a booth and told these sophisticated New York businessmen that we were heiresses from Minnesota, and though this was our first real trip to New York, we'd traveled "the Continent" a fair bit and so "of course" we'd flown through New York.

George found us absolutely fascinating, and wanted to know about everything we'd seen so far, and all the things we were planning to do while in Gotham. We told him we had tickets for *Annie* and *I Love My Wife*. But primarily, Julie said, "We want to shop."

Well, it turned out to be our lucky day, because George

was an investor in a number of different fashion-related businesses, and promised to help us out during our trip.

When George offered to take us out for dinner, Billy again tried to get out of it. George and Julie were getting quite cozy, but Billy seemed so repelled by me that my first instinct was to check myself for open running sores. I would have been happy if he'd just split, but George, and now Julie, insisted he accompany us. That's how we ended up at the French restaurant. Then at the disco. I couldn't remember all the places we'd gone after that, but Julie and I got back to the hotel really late, snoshed to the gills, fell asleep in our clothes, and slept until about four, when George called us.

Just as he said, George was well connected in the fashion and jewelry industries, and on subsequent days he took us in a limo to a bunch of designer showrooms in the garment district. When we walked in with him, people smiled and fell all over themselves to help us out. We were treated like princesses, given all kinds of great free stuff—clothes, jewelry, perfume—even had our pictures taken with two moderately famous designers, one of whom we recognized from the fashion credits in the back of *Mademoiselle* magazine. There were drinks at the Top of the Sixes, the Rainbow Room, and Windows on the World, jazz at Jimmy Ryan's, rides in carriages around Central Park, and so on.

You can imagine how dazzling this was to a couple of girls from a small town, sipping cocktails with swells in the Rainbow Room at the top of the RCA building, for instance, with the glittering jewel box of Manhattan out the window. The tallest building in Ferrous, at six stories, was the Hotel Grand (which also boasted the best restaurant, Filbert's), followed by the four-story MacCosham Professional Center, where most of the area doctors, dentists, plumbers, and chiropractors practiced. The main department store, MacCosham's, still called itself a dry-goods store, and though it was a good place to buy sheets, lawn-mowers, and licorice allsorts, the fashions sucked. People who cared about fashion bought their clothes in Duluth or Minneapolis–St. Paul.

So we ate New York up. I don't think we got more than four hours of sleep a night. We were, after all, in the city that never sleeps, where you can buy a saxophone at three in the morning. You can eat, drink, bowl, work out, buy groceries, pray in a church, hire a PI, mail a parcel to Bulgaria, get your windows cleaned, your pipes cleared, your spine aligned, your aquarium cleaned, an ancient Latin document translated, buy oxygen, and be tried and convicted twenty-four hours a day in this town. You used to be able to get your hair coiffed twenty-four hours a day too, but that place cut back its hours.

During that week, Julie went out with George every night, and I went out with them, and whichever of his handsome young friends he could dredge up for me, *almost* every night. What really struck us, or me at least, was how friendly everyone was to us. We were so popular. Men were constantly mistaking us for models.

Chuck and Lance came back from Florida tanned and swaggering with a few cheap souvenirs and a few more notches on their studly belts. Julie and I came back from New York with an extra suitcase each, bought at a Going Out of Business store in midtown just to carry all our free stuff home. But more than that, we came back changed.

After that trip, any glimpse of New York would set my heart soaring, from the opening credits of "All in the Family," "Rhoda," or "Taxi" to an on-location shoot-out scene between cops and drug dealers on "Kojak" reruns. Julie and I began to wonder if we couldn't be like the young Manhattan career women in *Mademoiselle* and *Vogue* who had glamorous jobs, furnished their tiny apartment kitchens in French provincial on an editorial assistant's salary, and transformed themselves effortlessly from Tailored Professional to Boldly Dressed Party Girl, against various Manhattan backdrops. We imagined a dynamic love life, different men every night, play openings, dinner with dashing ambassadors and princes. You too, Robin Hudson, can be an INTERNATIONAL BON VIVANT!

It had been such a great time, and seeing Chuck again was so anticlimactic. The men we met in New York were so exciting, and Chuck didn't seem to get my enthusiasm about New York. My visions of being married to and redeemed by him started fading, though they seemed to infect Chuck, who was suddenly saying he thought we should get married, and as soon as possible. Lance, though, was still intransigent on the marriage-to-Julie question, which confused her, because he had chased her for a long time before she finally went out with him. I figured he was playing hard to get. "But no matter," I said to her. "You don't need Lance."

When we did marry, the new daydream went, we would marry handsome big-city men (who would be completely supportive of our glamorous careers), live on Park Avenue, and have citified daughters whom we would take to revivals of *Annie*, followed by ice cream at Rumpelmayer's or Serendipity.

I can't have kids, so there was no Serafina Hudson-Whatever to eat ice cream at Serendipity with Ramona Goomey-Whatever. It made me wonder. I knew Julie had finally married Lance at the beginning of 1980 and moved to Ohio, only to get divorced a couple of years later. When her family packed up and left Ferrous for good, I lost track of Julie completely. Not that I hadn't thought about her a lot, and heard rumors. She was remarried and living in

Canada. She was working as a stripper in Vegas. She was in a mental institution in Florida. She was in jail for forgery in Texas, which seemed really unlikely, given her horrible handwriting. Something about Julie had always inspired a lot of gossip.

Was Julie remarried? Did she have kids? Even though she always talked about having kids, I had never pictured her with them. As a child, she was always forgetting her dolls at the playground, where they'd be scavenged by other kids, or torn apart by packs of wild dogs. Oh, wait. That was me.

And what about Billy and George? I'd thought about looking them up when I moved to New York but, remembering all the lies I'd told them, I didn't bother. By that time, disco was dead or dying and I was in J-school at NYU, hanging out with snotty bohos, filmmakers, actors, and so forth, interning in local television, smoking joints with my profs in Washington Square.

So much had happened to me since I'd last seen Julie. My God, I'd completely forgotten that I'd once dreamed of being a Park Avenue trophy wife. Gag. How differently my life turned out. What had happened to Julie? And what brought her back to New York?

✵ 6 ✵

"Goomey—that must have been a hard name to have as a kid," Tamayo said to me.

"Goony Goomey," I said, nodding. "That's the significance of the cootie catcher. We were both cootie girls. We had cooties."

"What are cooties?"

"Fleas, lice."

The subway platforms below the Port Authority, a major transfer point, were jammed with people, by my estimate about a quarter of them in costume, but, then again, in New York it is always so hard to tell.

The train came and the mobbed pressed on. An older black guy was sitting near the door, taking up an extra seat for his dinner, tuna out of a can, the lid pried open and rolled halfway back; a soft pretzel on a piece of wax paper; and a beer in a paper bag. I was tired and I wouldn't have minded a seat, so I fixed my best guilt-inducing stare on him. He looked up at me mildly amused and took a forkful of tuna and a bite of pretzel, washing it down with a swig of beer. He was in work clothes, probably had had a long day, and he was enjoying his meal so much nobody was going to begrudge him the extra seat, not even me.

A guy with an ax coming out of a big plastic wound in his head said, "This train stop at West 4th Street?"

"Yeah," the tuna-eating guy said.

"You had fleas?" Tamayo said to me. A few people around me inched away from me when she said that.

"These were figurative cooties. Didn't they have cooties

in Japan? Cootie girls, fleabags, whatever they were called in your schoolyard. The pariah kids."

"We didn't have cooties at my school, but we did have pariahs. I was one," Tamayo said.

"You were?"

"Yeah, me and this boy who had a very long head."

"Were you an official pariah? Or just a secret dork like most people?"

"I was a real pariah. The kids called me *gaijin*, which means 'barbarian,' because my dad was a foreigner, American, and then I had another name, which, translated, means 'bad-tempered girl with enormous feet.' "

"You have big feet?"

"Yeah, for a Japanese girl. I used to like to stomp the feet of the bullies when they were picking on me. Then I'd run like hell."

She lifted up the hem of her dress to show me her feet. She did have very large feet. I do too, size ten.

"Were you friends with the boy with the long head?" I said.

"God, no. We had nothing in common except that we were hated. Besides, the other kids made jokes about him and me marrying, and what ugly children we'd have, and so I didn't want to do anything that would associate me with him any more than we were already associated. I was a kid."

"Yeah, Julie and I didn't hang out much with the other cootie girl in our grade, Mabel. She was very quiet and always smelled like insecticide. We also avoided Francis, the cootie boy, like the plague. He was one of those little boys with slicked-back hair, a neatly pressed suit—short pants until junior high school—carried a briefcase. He got his revenge by becoming a hall monitor in junior high. He's now a CEO and a big Pat Buchanan contributor."

"The kid with the long head turned out badly. He joined the doomsday cult that planted the poison gas on the Tokyo subways."

"Kinda like Mabel. She became a born-again Christian for a while, dated a lot of substance abusers who looked like Jesus, and had a breakdown after one of them ripped off a liquor store and made his getaway in her Gremlin. The last I heard, she'd become a Moonie and married some Korean guy she knew for ten minutes in a mass wedding in San Francisco. Poor Mabel. But, then, maybe she's happy, or thinks she is."

"What's the difference? If you think you're happy you are. Ha-ha. You have cooties!"

"You're so mature."

"What did the kids call you?" she asked. "Carrot Top?"

"Red Knobby until eighth grade, when I developed the worst acne in my school. Then I was Lizard Lady for two years. Seems so funny now."

We got out at 23rd Street and Eighth Avenue, in Chelsea, or, as Claire once described it, the year-long festival of gorgeous unavailable men, since it is the new gay mecca.

The heat had subsided a bit, but it was still muggy, which made it clammy. On the next block, Sam Chinita glowed. A railway-style diner with hammered tin siding, bare-bones decor, and aqua-green curtains in the smallish windows, it specializes in Cuban-Chinese cuisine, which is fairly popular in New York, where hybrid cuisines like Cuban-Chinese and Mexican-French do well. There are lots of Jewish hybrids too, like kosher Chinese, kosher Italian, kosher Japanese, and kosher Indian.

While we waited for our crackling chicken with fried bananas and salad, Tamayo said, "The name on the handwritten note, Putli Bai, is that some kind of American girl thing?"

"She was an Indian bandit queen in the 1950s, a scarlet woman who led an army of bandits."

"Like the one in the movie *The Bandit Queen*?"

"That was Phoolan Devi, who came later, but the same idea. Julie read about Putli Bai somewhere when we were kids, and fell in love with the whole idea of her. It was a far cry better than being a cootie girl."

"I liked to pretend I was a pirate queen. That's a bandit queen, on water. I used one of my mom's knitting needles as a sword," Tamayo said, miming swordplay. "Tell me more about cooties."

Tamayo is obsessed with finding the America she saw from a distance, growing up in Japan—the America somewhere beyond *Life* magazine, American TV shows, the movies—and she has an endless appetite for stories about American childhood, especially American girlhood. She would sometimes try to describe my childhood for me, saying things like, "So, Sunday evening, when you and your family were sitting around the Philco watching Ed Sullivan . . ." For her last birthday, I gave her a book of North American girl songs and she got tears in her eyes and hugged me so hard I thought a lung had collapsed. You would have thought I'd just presented her with the Hope Diamond.

"What do you want to know?"

"Who decided who had cooties?"

"Mary MacCosham was the head arbiter at my school. What a bitch she was. Little Miss Perfect. But she had help in cootie allotment from Sis and Bobby Fanning. They made me a cootie girl at the end of first grade and made Julie one when she moved to Ferrous in fifth grade. Imagine having that kind of power."

I took out a pen and drew a round dot on her arm, with the initials "C.S." beneath it.

"This is a cootie shot," I said. "The other kids had to get cootie shots to protect them from our cooties, in case they bumped up against one of us during fire drill or in the cloakroom."

You couldn't give yourself a cootie shot, I explained. You had to get it from someone else, so it was imperative to find someone who could give you a cootie shot as soon as you got to school, before you had contact with any cootie kids. Because, if you got cooties from a cootie kid, you'd be a cootie kid too, at least temporarily.

"And what did kids do if they got temporary cooties? Was there a ritual delousing?"

"Yeah. They went to Mary, Sis, or Bobby and got one of them to remove the cooties with a paper cootie catcher, like the one Candy saw in the envelope."

"Like those monkeys who pick lice off each other."

"Kind of, yeah."

When I hear people say children are naturally "sweet and innocent" I think, Excuse me?!? Were you ever a child? Or did you just land here from Mars, or some other planet where children really are naturally sweet and innocent? Alone, kids are sweet. Put two or more of them together and it changes the equation. Children are a little primitive society all their own, with their own leaders, dictators, cops, rules, punishments, uniformity, and papal indulgences. Sweet and innocent, sure, SOMETIMES, and ignorant and helpless, and cruel too. Which is why you have to watch the little buggers like hawks. If they're so naturally sweet and innocent, how come so many of them grow up to be shitty adults? Do the shitty adults turn the kids bad, or do bad kids just naturally grow up into shitty adults? I guess it's a chicken-or-egg thing. Made me think about a saying I saw on a T-shirt in Central Park, "Search your soul . . . find your inner child . . . and then give it a good smack."

I'm against smacking, but I thought the shirt made a good point.

"But Mary and her gang would never remove your cooties," Tamayo said.

"No, so Julie and I made our own cootie catchers, and before class, we'd remove each other's cooties. That way, it theoretically didn't matter as much what the other kids said, because *we* knew we didn't have cooties."

"At my school the arbiter of social rank was Neiko Hatsumoto. What an asshole. She tried to push me out a window once."

"God, that's terrible."

"And she and some of her acolytes followed me home and tried to push me into the river once."

"Jesus. Mary MacCosham stopped a little short of attempted murder. Did you do anything to get back at them? Other than stomping their feet."

"No. I just ignored them and changed schools as soon as I could get into the school I wanted, when I was ten. I didn't care so much that I was a pariah, because I thought the bullies were idiots anyway, but some kids in Japan get driven off the deep end by bullying. Anyway, I come from a long line of rebellious women, like my funny mother, and her funny mother."

"What happened to Neiko Hatsumoto?"

"She's dead," Tamayo said matter-of-factly. "She was blown into the Sea of Japan during Typhoon Vernon in 1993. What happened to Mary?"

"Oddly enough, she moved to New York too. Married some Harvard boy from a bankrupt, distaff branch of the Astor clan, and they moved to the Upper East Side. They got divorced in a big scandal a couple of years ago. Well, it wasn't much of a scandal here. I heard about it back home, where it was huge."

According to my reliable sources, Mary had had a motherfucker of a midlife crisis. Her husband caught her in flagrante delecto with the guy who was supposed to be installing a sauna, and in the divorce he also named a plumber, a pizza delivery boy, and a cab driver. In the settlement, he got custody of the kids and she had to pay him alimony and child support.

Mary MacCosham. Even now, thinking of her sent a rat up my trouser leg, as Mike likes to say. Pretty in a thin, blonde, stick-up-the-ass, finger-down-the-throat kind of way, she came from one of the two richest families in my hometown.

"She lives here? Have you ever talked to her?" Tamayo said.

"Hell, no. I saw her on the street once, a few years before her motherfucker of a midlife crisis, but I didn't speak to her."

At first, I hadn't recognized Mary, because she had a different nose and bigger tits. But then I saw the woman she was with was her mother. I hadn't seen old Mrs. MacCosham in a few years, but she looked much the same, even though surgery had probably kept her that way. When they walked away, I knew for sure it was them, because they both suffered from a psychological disorder known as symmetromania—their movements were always perfectly timed and symmetrical. It was funny the way they walked. Mary started out walking to her own gait, but after a few strides, she fell into her mother's painfully exact rhythm.

"Mary's kind of a failed socialite now. In Ferrous, she was a princess. In Manhattan, she's much further down the peerage," I said, and Tamayo smiled. She seemed to take a strange satisfaction in Mary's misery.

Our food arrived. I called home on the off chance that Kathy had called, and there was one new message, this one from my very occasional boyfriend Eric. He wanted to know if I got his postcard—I hadn't—and said he'd called earlier but the machine was off. He was in Seattle, at the airport, and would be stopping over in New York for the weekend on his way to see his mom in Florida, and he wanted to hang out Saturday and Sunday.

"*Pee-Wee's Big Adventure*, a bottle of vodka, and thou?" he suggested. That would have sounded so good any time but right now.

"Shit," I said, slamming the phone shut.

"What is it?" Tamayo asked, through a mouthful of crackling chicken.

"Eric's coming to town. Fuck."

"But you like him."

"Mike and Eric are *both* going to be here this weekend. Everything is going wrong today. And everything had been going so . . . okay lately."

"If Eric and Mike are both here, who will you spend the weekend with?"

"I don't know, that's the problem."

"Can't you see both of them?" Tamayo said.

"Too *Jules and Jim*."

"Yeah, it hardly ever works in real life," Tamayo said wistfully. "A young Tibetan woman I met, a film student, she says that in her culture women are allowed to have up to three husbands."

"Is there a catch?"

"They're supposed to be brothers. But according to Indra, women of her generation take a broad view of fraternity. All men are brothers under the skin."

"How do they get the men to go along with that?" I asked.

"I didn't get a chance to ask her that. How do you?"

"Well, I only see one at a time, and I don't date married

men or brothers. We all know we see other people, but we don't ask and don't tell about other people we see, we use condoms, and the guys I date spend most of their time out of town."

Men, I love 'em, but on a full-time basis they cramp my style. Cautious nonmonogamy suits me better, but it's a lot harder than it looks. In order to pull it off, you have to have a fear of commitment slightly greater than your desire for emotional security, kind of like the gravitational hammock on Planet Tamayo. Once you get the right balance there, you have to reach some honest understanding with the men involved, without going into detail or drawing up a contract.

Then you get into the logistics problem, which had actually resolved itself very easily for me, once I stopped dating guys who lived in New York all the time. That way, you avoid embarrassing situations, like being out at a bar with some cute Coast Guard cadet and running into a doctor you recently shagged. For example. Boy, can that make you feel slutty. Which I wasn't, not really, except for a brief period the year before, when, as they say, I "embraced my freedom" and had a few adventures. Now I had one sometime boyfriend, Mike, and a few occasional boyfriends, including Eric, my postdivorce transitional man. Sometimes I felt guilty, because some women have no men and here I was, making a pig of myself with several.

Yeah, the logistics hadn't been much of a problem. Until now. Eric or Mike, Mike or Eric. Yikes. I didn't get to see Eric that often, which may be why we always had a really great time when we did see each other. In the last year I'd seen him twice—for one week in New York, while Mike was in Central America shooting a rain forest documentary, and for a long weekend in London. Things were very loose and easy with both Mike and Eric, which made this dilemma more difficult. It meant making a *decision* and taking the *responsibility* and the *consequences.*

"Talk to Sally. Call her and leave a message on her machine. It can't hurt," Tamayo said.

"I'm glad Sally is helpful to you, but . . ." I stopped myself before I finished the sentence and said that Sally is an insane woman whose life is a mess, and who blames it all on bad karma accumulated when she was a promiscuous senatrix in ancient Rome or a murderous Sumerian harlot. There was a lot my other friends didn't know about Sally, which I couldn't tell them because it would mean betraying Sally's confidences. This being-a-good-friend stuff was a helluva lot trickier than I thought it would be.

Besides, I already knew what Sally would say about my love life. For a bald woman with a scorpion tattoo up the back of her skull who burned herbs in a little black iron cauldron, Sally gave shockingly conventional advice about love. She believed in monogamy and marriage—for everyone!—and above all she believed in The Madness.

"Sally is a flawed mortal and she can't predict the future. Or the past," I said.

"She can tell the future, in a way. She has a way of finding out what you really want, you know, articulating the voice in your heart. I bet she'd have something to say about this Julie business too. She can help you see what it is you really want to do, and that reinforces it somehow," Tamayo said. "Makes it come true."

"Maybe what people want to do isn't what they need to do, or are capable of doing. I mean, people can be very easily manipulated, and they could be led into making big mistakes. I had a cab driver today who is convinced someone put a curse on him and his penis is disappearing."

"That's called Shook Yang syndrome," Tamayo said.

"It's a, what do you call it, mass hysteria not uncommon in Asia. It was unheard of until some quack in China two hundred years ago wrote a medical book and included it. Then men all over Asia started succumbing to it."

"See how dangerous the power of suggestion is?" I said. I try to keep an open mind and I understand, with the millennium approaching, that people are looking for answers from traditional and nontraditional sources, Jesus, Buddha, dead ancestors, Eleanor Roosevelt, Nostradamus, aliens, etc. But I knew way too much about Sally to take her seriously.

"The power of suggestion isn't dangerous if you know how to use it," Tamayo said. "Take sigils."

"Sigils?"

"Yeah, they're short sentences stating your wishes. You take out every repeating letter, rewrite it, stare at it until you have memorized the result, then you burn the piece of paper, or throw it away, and try to forget what you wrote. The message is now lodged in your subconscious, and your subconscious will guide you towards making your dreams come true."

"Right, gotta go the . . ."

". . . microchip in your buttocks is beeping. Yeah yeah yeah. It may sound insane, but it's really a kind of self-hypnosis. Write down: I will find Julie." She wrote it on a paper napkin for me, and then crossed out the repeating letters, so it looked like "IwlfndJu."

"IwilfundJu," I read, phonetically. "Isn't that a Hasidic Lewis Carroll character?"

"Laugh, but now it is lodged in your subconscious. If you're so skeptical, why did you hire Sally to consult on your special report on the paranormal?

"To get her point of view, not to give her beliefs credibility," I said. The real reason I hired Sally was to help restore her confidence after a period of intense crisis. My intentions were good. I don't know why I felt so guilty and so responsible for Sally. It wasn't my fault her last beauregard had taken a flyer with $5,000 of her money, leaving no forwarding address, and leaving her in tremendous debt. As if that wasn't enough, her cat, Pie, who had been with her since freshman year at Princeton, died.

All this sparked her major tailspin and crisis of faith, because nothing in her charts or readings of the tarot had predicted it. She stopped taking clients, fell behind in her rent. Unable to "prognosticate," grieving for Pie, letting the bills pile up, virtually unemployable because of her appearance and attitude, she thought she was left with only two options, bankruptcy court or faking her own death. Then Sally found a different option, and went to work as a human trial subject for experimental drugs, which resulted in a number of unpleasant side effects.

Since the paranormal series, she'd been getting back in the swing of things, which had, at first, made me feel good, because I'd been a good friend and helped her get her confidence back. Now I was feeling kind of shitty, now that a couple of my friends were consulting Sally and actually taking her advice.

"Did you ever play space girl when you were a kid?" Tamayo asked, snapping me back to the conversation. She waved at the waiter for the check.

"Not very often, but I bet you did."

" 'Star Voyager Tamayo,' my own private television series. In this episode, every episode, Star Voyager Tamayo encounters aliens who want to take over the world."

"Did you defeat them in every episode?"

"Most, not all. Sometimes the aliens were smarter and having more fun, so I joined them in taking over the world, until worse aliens came along and tried to take it over from us."

"Julie is going to love you," I said. Then I had a very childish thought. I hoped Julie didn't like Tamayo better than she liked me.

❖ 7 ❖

"LOOK! A LAUGHER," Tamayo said, as we left Chinita.

A man was standing in the purple neon light radiating from a closed dry cleaner's, laughing at everyone who went past, regardless of whether they were in costume or not.

"A lot of nuts out tonight. That's the first random laugher I've seen since spring," Tamayo said, referring to the season when the city's insane are lighthearted and tend to tear through the streets laughing at everything. I've felt like that myself a time or two, though not nearly often enough.

"He has a great laugh, doesn't he?" she marveled. With a kind of resigned horror, I watched as she ran up to the laughing man.

"Why did the chicken cross the road?" she said to him. "To get to the other side."

The man laughed.

"Benadryl Allergy Medicine," Tamayo said.

The man thought this was equally funny.

"Which came first, the chicken or the egg?" she went on, waiting for an answer as though it were a formality. "Because there was no more pudding."

The man laughed hysterically at her non sequitur, while I tugged her away.

"You shouldn't play with the insane that way," I said.

"He's harmless."

"Maybe, maybe not. I've got a clipping at home about two barbers who were killed in an argument with two other men over which came first, the chicken or the egg. No shit. You can't be too careful."

"His laughter was so *pure*. I'd love to take that guy to a comedy club."

I yawned, not at Tamayo, but because I was tired and thinking about all the work I had waiting once I found Julie and Kathy. I had reports due, laundry, checks to write, a boyfriend to choose, and I had to make my apartment man-ready, i.e., change the sheets, stock the fridge, and put the toilet seat up.

"Hasn't that vitamin kicked in yet?" Tamayo said.

"Not yet."

"You're not turning into a square, are you?"

"No, more of a fullerene."

I was struck by how young Tamayo was, and I don't just mean in the ageless way common among people who live outside the normal space/time continuum. She was hovering around thirty, and she still had boundless energy and the insane belief that all people have something good in them and anything was possible.

All my friends, the ones I hung with more or less regularly, were either younger than me or older than me, and so there were a lot of areas where we didn't quite jibe. My younger friends had different expectations, different cultural milestones, a slightly different collective point of view, as did my older friends.

My friends my own age and my college girlfriends, alas, those same girls who impressed me with their cheerful amorality when I first moved to New York, were now married, homeowning, bridge- and golf-playing mothers, in the Junior League, or—no shit—the DAR. It was like they were growing older in a parallel universe. Maybe, in some other parallel universe, I too had a husband and a home and kids.

But in this universe, they were lost to me in many subtle ways, pulled away by their own busy lives. Julie, I hoped, could be found again. Just as Phil and Helen found some common history only they understood, Julie and I had that too. A lot of it.

We picked up the parade at Sixth and 18th, a grand stretch of old dry-goods stores known as Ladies' Mile. Back at the turn of the century, Ladies' Mile was where gentlemen dropped their wives while they headed a few blocks over to the Tenderloin to gamble and gambol with women who were not considered "ladies." Now it's the closest thing we have in Manhattan to a mall, with one chain store after another from 23rd Street to 16th, where the "mall" ends at the New York Foundling Hospital.

Behind the blue police barricades lining the parade route, the people were ten deep. As my luck would have it, all the tall people were near the front. We could hardly move, and all I could see were the tops of some floats.

"Come on," Tamayo said, taking my hand and leading me through the crunch to the front of the barricades. She ducked under the barricade when the nearby cop was turned away, and I followed. We walked against the parade stream, through a group of people dressed as various New York buildings in a walking skyline. Two guys in a cow costume came past us, followed by a man in a white coat holding a big butterfly net.

"Mad cow, get it?" Tamayo hollered back at me.

We skirted around the gay high-school marching band, led by what looked in this light like a forty-year-old male majorette in white go-go boots and red spangled hot pants. Probably the math teacher. But he did twirl a good baton.

A mermaid in a glass aquarium drifted by. Two giant red high-heeled shoes, about six feet tall, clomped past. A float bearing a bunch of muscle men approached, blasting out the Bangles' song "Walk Like an Egyptian."

Tamayo danced alongside. One of the muscle men reached down and hoisted her onto the float, which bore the legend, in gold, silver, and green tinsel, "The 52 Sons of Ramses."

"Robin, I'll catch up with you laterrr . . ." Tamayo called, waving, disappearing. That's Tamayo, always getting swept up in parades, going where the breeze blows her, and somehow making out more than just okay. Not long ago, things hadn't been going so well for Tamayo. A trip back to Japan resulted in her being publicly denounced in the Japanese Diet because of some rude jokes she made about Japanese Diet members, sumo wrestlers, and their assorted sexual habits. Right after that, she lost a network-development deal that was given to a "nicer" Japanese girl comic, Noriko Mori. Tamayo got depressed, but even when she was depressed, she managed to laugh. She didn't get the blues like other people. If I had to ascribe a color to Tamayo's melancholy, it would be lavender.

Oh well, I thought as she faded into a dot in the distance, I can make better time without her for now.

I got out of the parade on 13th Street, and as soon as I did I realized my phone was ringing in my purse.

"Hello?" I said, sticking a finger in my free ear to block out the parade noise behind me.

"I can't hear you!" I shouted. "Call me back in . . ."

I was heading down Fifth to Washington Square Park and wouldn't be able to duck into a quiet place until West 3rd Street.

"FIFTEEN MINUTES!" I shouted, and hung up.

It took me almost fifteen minutes just to get through Washington Square, once a graveyard, also a popular place for hanging criminals, and now the heart of NYU and Greenwich Village. The square was packed with folks in costume, cops, and people hawking things, from hot dogs to marijuana. By the statue of Garibaldi, I had to squeeze past a guy who was holding a big stick full of Ariel the Little Mermaid dolls. I wondered if you could kill someone with a stick full of mermaid dolls.

"Oh, Joey!" one young girl with a distinctly New York accent shrilled above the din. "Stop, Joey! You're killin' me." Near the bocce court, a boy with a big ring through his nose was nose-kissing a laughing girl with pierced eyebrows, which looked to me like an ugly accident waiting to happen.

What will kids do next? I thought. I hear some get branded—you know, with hot irons. Still, these two looked kind of sweet and hormonal, in the full grip of The Madness. What brought them together, I wondered, and what would tear them apart? Kids. So cynical, this younger generation, and yet they still fall in love.

On West 3rd, I found a Korean greengrocer, a bright circle of light on the corner, with the typical alfresco fruit display, oranges, limes, apples, melons—bright colors gleaming in the darkness, like Aladdin's cave of jewels. I popped in and got an Evian, very efficiently snatching it out of the cooler and plopping it down with two bucks on the counter. The greengrocer ignored me. He was looking out the door at a parked car and a man who was studying the front tire closely.

"Wait for it," he whispered to me.

The man bent over and tried to grab something stuck halfway under the tire. After several tries, he stomped off cursing.

The grocer burst into laughter.

"It's a ten-dollar bill. I put it there," he said to me, and winked. He laughed some more and took my money.

What people do to amuse themselves. I swear to God, everyone in this city is nuts.

The Backslash was on Bleecker, just down from where it meets MacDougal, aka Coffeehouse Junction because there is a coffeehouse on every corner of this intersection. It was coming back to me. We had come to this place after the disco with George and Billy, when it was Cafe Buñuel. Julie had read about it in one of the magazines, or seen it in the background of a fashion layout or something. It was an old-time, beatniky Greenwich Village place where you imagined a bunch of goateed guys in berets and black turtlenecks discussing The Bomb and Burroughs with pale girls in black capri pants. When Julie and I went there in 1979, it was bereft of berets, but something of that atmosphere still lingered.

Now it was an Internet café, essentially a coffeehouse with computers. Patrons get a java and sit down in front of a computer screen to go online, interacting not with each other, but with folks in cyberspace. It was weird, quiet, just the hum of computers, the click of mice, and the squoosh of the cappuccino machine. Very spooky and antisocial.

After getting me a coffee and asking me the skill-testing question—"Who was Hummer High's Athlete of the Year in 1975?"—the languid young man behind the ornate antique cash register handed me an envelope. This time, the skill-testing question wasn't about me, not directly. The answer was: Doug Gribetz. Kathy wouldn't know this answer.

"Someone else was in asking about the envelope," the young man said.

"Who?"

"A woman in a green wig and Groucho glasses, but she couldn't answer the question," he said.

"Hmmm. Thanks," I said, and took my coffee to a little round marble table.

Inside the envelope, there was another cootie catcher, a photo, and half a dollar bill. The typed note inside the cootie catcher said, "Wait for contact." That was it.

The half dollar bill had French handwriting on it. George had spoken to me in French again here, and at that point, to cover my ass, I'd told him that I read French better than I spoke it, though I did neither. He wrote something on a dollar bill and handed it to me.

"What does it say?" Billy had asked.

"May all your dreams come true," George had said. "It's good luck."

After nodding stupidly, as if I knew what he'd written, I took the dollar and put it in my purse. George said something else to me in French, and when I didn't answer, he winked again, and started talking in English. The thing about the dollar bill was, later that night, when we got back to the hotel, I ripped it in half and gave half to Julie so we could each have some of the good luck contained therein. The plan was, we would tape the dollar together the next time we came to New York and spend it on something for both of us. Somehow, we believed this would activate the good luck and make our wishes come true.

Now I had a little French under my belt, and I could read the partial sentence on this half-dollar.

"Il essaie . . ." it said. He is trying.

How strange. I wondered what the second half of the dollar bill said. I had it tucked away somewhere.

The photo, which showed Julie with George in front of the old Cafe Buñuel, stopped me cold. I looked more closely at it. You know how sometimes you see a movie you first saw a long time ago, and you recognize a now famous actor in it? When you watched it the first time, he or she was unknown, and so he or she didn't really register with you. The supporting or minor character played by the now famous person appears larger, and the movie takes on a whole different dimension.

Well, that's how I felt when I looked at the photo. I recognized George from somewhere other than that night, somewhere since. George was smiling broadly for the camera, his arm around Julie.

The photo was of poor quality, but as I remembered it, both George and Billy were good-looking in a swarthy kind of way, George a bit taller with distinctive flaring nostrils, Billy a bit plumper with a piggy nose. I couldn't be sure. There were no pictures of Billy, and I couldn't for the life of me fix his face in my mind.

A couple of years after that trip, when I was older and wiser, etc., I figured that Billy was camera-shy because he was probably married. He didn't wear a ring, but lots of men didn't, and don't, even today.

Now I wondered if Billy wasn't secretly gay. Though he didn't look gay—he was macho to the nth—a lot of gay guys I know don't look or act "gay," and some latent gays overcompensate with hypermasculinity. Billy stuck to George like glue, and was more interested in watching him on the dance floor than watching me, and they went to the men's room together a few times. Wow. I'd never thought about it before, but now I figured either they were doing coke in the john, or Billy was trying to cop an ogle at the urinals or something.

Come to think of it, George must have picked up on that weird vibe from Billy too, I thought. At Cafe Buñuel, he had whispered something in Julie's ear before he went to the men's room, and when Billy tried to get up, Julie pulled him down, put her arm through his, and said, "Don't desert us!" We held him there, laughing. We thought it was a big game.

Of course, I couldn't tell then that either or both of them were gay. I didn't know the Village People were gay stereotypes until I had been living in New York for about six months and one of my college friends told me, that's how naïve I was.

Wait for contact, said the typed "clue." Contact would be helpful, since I hadn't a clue where to go next. I remembered a lot of things we did on that trip, but I didn't remember exactly when we did them. Time and geography blend together after the passage of years. Even my ex, Burke, and his fiancée, Gwen, after knowing each other just under a year, confused their memories of shared events. At dinner in L.A., they told a story about their European vacation and had to keep referring to each other during their joint storytelling—"What day did we get stuck behind the long line of turnip trucks?" "In Slovakia, after we took that wrong turn?" "Yeah." "Monday, Tuesday, the same day we lost the muffler on the Skoda." "No no, we lost the muffler in Prague. . . ."

Another reason I didn't remember that evening as clearly as I should, aside from the passage of time and all the wine spritzers, was that I was so self-conscious, so focused on not giving myself away in the face of all our big old lies, that I didn't pay attention to a lot of other stuff going on.

Where the hell did we go next? I remembered Julie and George whooping it up on Bleecker Street and Julie asserting at the top of her lungs that she wasn't tired. "I'll sleep when I'm dead," she said, her motto du jour. This was, after all, the city that never sleeps, and we were young. George put his arm around Julie and they giggled, while the morose Billy and I walked behind them in silence.

Shortly after, as I recalled, some friends of George and Billy's arrived and Billy left with them, while George, Julie, and I continued on.

Next . . . next. I wracked my brain. Was it the . . . the Staten Island Ferry? Yeah, we'd taken the ferry for the ride past the Statue of Liberty at 3 A.M. There were hardly any people aboard, and we drank coffee out of paper cups with one of the ferry engineers, who showed us pictures from his last vacation at a nudist colony.

No, that was the night I went out with Ricardo, a disco promoter I met in the hotel lobby, and Julie went out alone with George. Ricardo was back in his hometown for the big disco convention. Though Julie was anxious about him—"He's Puerto Rican or black or something, you don't even know him"—I took up his offer to go out because he'd made me laugh in the lobby and seemed like a nice guy . . . and I was sick of hanging around with Julie and George, who only had eyes for each other. Ricardo took me to eat at a Brooklyn diner called the Blue Bird Diner, then we went back to Manhattan to a disco in Spanish Harlem. I was the whitest person there, which was strange for me, coming from a pigmentless part of the nation, but nobody made it a problem for me, even though I was with a dark-skinned man. *Au contraire.* Everyone was really friendly. Anyway, we ended the night on the Staten Island Ferry. That was my third or fourth night in New York.

If only we hadn't had so much to drink that second night . . .

"Are you Robin Hudson?"

I looked up. A woman in a green wig and Groucho-nose glasses was looking down at me. It wasn't Kathy.

"Yes."

"Are you looking for Kathy?" she said, with a heavy New York accent.

"Yeah."

"Come with me," she said.

Contact.

"Where are we going?" I said.

"Up to the corner of LaGuardia Place," she said. "This won't take long."

"And who are you?" I said to the woman. "Are you a friend of Julie's?"

She just smiled at me.

When we got to LaGuardia and Bleecker, also known as the corner of Walk and Don't Walk because there used to be a tavern by that name on this corner, the green-haired woman said, "Cross over to that lot."

She was pointing to a little parking area in front of a strip of shops. There was a black car parked there.

We crossed and she said, "Get in the car."

A voice in my head said, "Never get into cars with strangers." But I hesitated only for a moment because this was just so Julie-esque.

✳ 8 ✳

THE CAR DOOR OPENED, and I slid into the back seat. In the shadowy car, there were three more women in green wigs and Groucho-nose glasses. The woman who had walked me over slid in behind me. The car was heavy with the smell of Shalimar.

The woman to my left, apparently the head woman, said, "Kathy is fine."

"Thanks for letting me know. I was a bit worried. I'm very anxious to find her."

"Good," the woman said. She turned to the bewigged woman in the front and said, "Let's get out of here."

The car pulled out into the street. About three feet later it stopped. Traffic was really bad.

"Did Julie dream up those outfits, or did you?" I said.

"Julie?" she said, with an odd, perplexed note in her voice. "No, I did."

Yeah, I should have guessed that. Their costumes were strictly off the rack, cheap polymer wigs and the kind of nose glasses you can buy in any convenience store in New York on Halloween. If Julie had done the costumes, she would have made them bearded ladies or Jehovah's Witnesses. If Julie had done them as Groucho, who is one of my personal heroes, they would look like authentic, quality Grouchos. Or she would have made each of them a different Marx brother, and put them in dresses, made them the Marx Sisters. She had imagination.

"Are you actors she hired, or friends of Julie's?" I asked.

The head woman looked at me coldly. "Actors," she fairly snapped at me.

Touchy, jeez. It's so easy to offend some people.

"Sorry, I didn't mean to block the action or ruin the fun or whatever," I said. "Are you going to give me a clue?"

The car drove forward again, stopping after a block.

"Yeah, we've got a clue for you," the woman to my left said. "This is the skill-testing question: When did you last speak to Julie Goomey?"

She lit a cigarette and exhaled in my direction.

Her accent was hard to place. I couldn't tell if she normally had an upper-class accent and was affecting the borough accent or vice versa, if she was trying to do either Marisa Tomei in *My Cousin Vinnie* or Bette Davis in *All About Eve*.

"Nineteen seventy-nine," I said.

"What did the last clue say?"

"Wait for contact."

"Contact. Uh-huh," she said, and dragged on her cigarette. "The clue is to go to the next place, and don't quit until you find Granny."

"Granny!" I laughed in spite of myself. "Then you're going to load up the truck and head to Beverleee? Look, you're probably a great actress and you'd rather be doing *Uncle Vanya* than this. But, you see, I'm tired. If you know where I'm supposed to go next, please tell me."

There was silence, then she said, "We don't know where you're supposed to go next. We're just here to keep an eye on you."

"All right. So, when I find Granny . . ."

"You just bring her to us, and we'll look after the rest," she said, sounding kind of pissed. "You have until dawn. I have your cell-phone number, I'll be calling you, and we'll be watching you."

"Did you call me about half an hour ago?"

"No. Someone else called you about this?"

"Possibly. I couldn't hear over the parade."

"I'm not supposed to tell you this, but you're going to be . . . tested, like. Others may ask you about Julie Goomey," the head woman said, exhaling cigarette smoke as she did. "Do not give them any information. If you do, you blow everything."

"Thanks," I said. "I appreciate that. I'm not as young as I used to be. I can't keep up with Julie's byzantine games anymore."

"I understand," said the head woman.

She sounded older than me, but maybe it was just because she was tired too, or "acting." She hadn't done a very good job, but what can you expect? What a sucky life that can be, being an actor in New York, having to support yourself temping or waitressing, doing singing telegrams and dressing up like a chicken to hand out brochures to people outside McDonald's. I knew lots of people who did it in college, some very successful now, and it was all just part of the adventure to them. But they were young then. Probably the adventure of it wears off by the time you hit forty and are still standing outside McDonald's on a sweltering day in a chicken suit.

How could they know that for her pranks Julie was legendary—in her mind, in mine, and in those of her other coconspirators and victims? You had to get up pretty early in the morning not to fall for Julie's stunts. This one reminded me of the time we enlisted the drama club to send the Valhalla High football team and pep squad on that wild-goose chase, while we, with the help of several boys and a van, stole the Valhalla mascot, the Iron Maiden. The Iron Maiden was a plaster-of-paris statue of a woman, kneeling, her mouth in a beseeching O. When she was found the next morning, she was placed facing our mascot, the god Vulcan, who was standing. The maiden's beseeching O was at Vulcan's crotch level, making it look from twenty feet away like she was giving him a blow job. Vulcan's Hummer. It was Julie who saw the Iron Maiden and envisioned the tableau, Julie who persuaded the drama club to take part. She gave participants only a piece of the puzzle, though, not the whole thing, so no one party could reveal the extent of the conspiracy. Oh, if only Richard Nixon had known Julie Goomey.

Finally, the car stopped, and I got out at Broadway and Broome Street, down in SoHo, and I waved goodbye to the green-wigged, mustachioed women.

Which way to go? If it hadn't been for Kathy, I would have canned the whole thing and gone home, figuring Julie could bloody well call me on the telephone like a sane person if she wanted to mend our fences. But, poor Kathy, she was probably sitting somewhere with Julie, waiting patiently for me, bored. If I was lucky she was bored. Possibly, she was being lavishly entertained by Julie's embarrassing stories about me. Julie knew some good ones, things even I don't care to admit to, like the time Julie made me laugh so hard in sixth-grade assembly that I peed in my pants, which everyone in the school saw. Or the time I was cheerleading during an important high-school football game and I wiped out in a big mud puddle. Even the fact that I was a cheerleader was something I'd omitted in the c.v. I recited to Kathy. (I only became a cheerleader because it seemed to me that boys especially liked girls who stayed on the sidelines and cheered them on, and I liked boys a *lot.*)

Kathy looked up to me and I liked that. I wasn't used to it. There were so many ways Julie could shake the image of me I'd carefully constructed for Kathy, the efficient, mature, self-made executive image.

Okay, I admit, I had another reason to keep going, aside from Kathy. I wanted to solve this one. Julie was always so much better at this kind of thing than me. I'd never quite forgiven her for solving Rubik's Cube in ten tries.

On Broadway, I looked one way, then the next, but had no idea in which direction to go. Someone dressed as Munch's *The Scream* stopped me and asked me if I knew where West Broadway was. I felt like she looked. She was an out-of-towner, she said, thought West Broadway was just a particular side of Broadway, and didn't know it was a whole separate street. I pointed the way and watched her walk away, past a scavenger pushing a huge cart full of stuff down the middle of the street, looking like a World War II refugee. I don't think he was in costume. Ever since the city installed pinkish street lamps, the streets downtown have looked like one of those after-dark Brassaï photographs of 1930s Paris.

We weren't in SoHo that second night in New York, I was fairly certain of that. Little Italy? That struck enough of a chord that I headed in that direction.

Walking down Mulberry, I looked up and down every cross street. At Mulberry and Grand, and just down the street a little, I saw Funnicula, which struck a chord, the wrong chord. I'd gone there with Burke, when we were both young reporters covering the Lonnie Katz murder trial. Every night, after we filed our reports, we went there to soak up the atmosphere and fall in love. I thought about going in for a moment, but it would be too weird, now that Burke was in love with Gwen. Maybe they'll come here, I thought. Maybe not. They've found new places that belong just to them. They've started a new history. Funnicula was lost now to both of us.

Damn, that made me feel sad, even though there were good reasons why our marriage broke up and I couldn't see us together again. As they say, nothing finalizes divorce like remarriage. I kept walking down Mulberry, passing festive strangers who were a little drunk and laughing. If you're not in the right mood, the laughter of strangers can be a tad depressing, so I looked away. My eye caught on a little clump of red, green, and white tinsel stuck in a chain-link fence, glittering in the streetlight, left over from the Feast of San Gennaro, in September. For some reason, that pathetic piece of tinsel made me feel even sadder.

A little farther along Mulberry, I looked down Hester Street and saw Fonsecci's. Immediately, I recognized the name and the sign, a vertical green neon sign, like a down word in a crossword puzzle. Against the dark sky, you couldn't see the supports anchoring the sign to the building, so it looked like it was floating in the night air. This was the place.

This time when I walked in, I felt a chill. Unlike so many stops on this route, Fonsecci's hadn't changed much, and for some reason, I found that even more disorienting than Chez Biftek and Joy II. It was a dark place, redolent of cigars and floozy perfume, with a bar, a small empty stage, and a dozen round tables surrounded by deep armchairs, about half of them empty.

"I'm here to pick up the clue left for me in the charity murder mystery," I said to the man standing behind the bar.

"Huh?" he said. He went to find someone who would know what the hell I was talking about. When he came back, he said, "If something was left, nobody on this shift knows anything about it. Maybe the evening shift, but I doubt any of them are reachable tonight."

"Shit," I said. "I mean, thanks anyway."

I gave him my card and, just for the hell of it, I ordered a wine spritzer and silently toasted Julie for managing to screw up my night completely.

Was I remembering wrong? We'd been in Little Italy twice, the second night we were in New York, and the last night, when we came down here with George and Gabriel, the guy he'd coerced into being my escort. Gabriel was a male model, or so he said, with what I believe are now called Jeri curls. I didn't remember much about Gabriel, except that he and I didn't click and he split his tight black silk pants on the dance floor later while doing an unintentional Tony Manero imitation.

Maybe we'd been here the last night. No, I thought, the last night we'd come down here for dinner at Angelo's. We were definitely at Fonsecci's the second night.

So lost in thought was I that I barely noticed a man had sat down on the stool next to me.

"Excuse me," he whispered. "Are you looking for Julie Goomey?"

Contact.

"Yes."

"So am I," he said, still whispering, flashing his badge, which identified him as a special agent, "Jeff Walter," with the FBI. A friend of mine has authentic-looking FBI ID from working as an extra on "The X-Files," and this looked a lot less authentic. The picture was ever so slightly crooked and there was a tiny air bubble between his picture and the lamination.

This guy was straight from Central Casting, a tall, clean-cut-looking white guy who kinda reminded me of this poor Mormon missionary who did his service in Five Towns and was unwittingly involved in a few of Julie's high-school pranks.

Guess he doesn't know it's against the law to impersonate an FBI agent, I thought. "I wouldn't flash that badge around here too much if I were you," I said.

He was about to say something and I said, "Look, if you

know where she is, I hope you'll tell me. I'm tired. My night is completely fucked up, I have a big problem in my personal life. My intern is no doubt hearing all sorts of terribly embarrassing stories about me and will never respect me again and I have a report due Monday morning."

"So you haven't seen Julie. . . ."

"I haven't seen her since 1979," I said, then remembered what the wig-wearing women had said about not giving information, about being tested.

"Can you tell me what you know about Julie, how you came to be involved?"

"I don't know a damn thing. I bet you know more than I do," I said.

"Why did she send me here to meet you? I've been waiting here for three hours. I finally called your place of employment, and your assignment desk gave me your cellular number, but I don't think your phone is working, because you couldn't hear me."

"You're the one who called. How did Julie contact you?"

"I got a FedEx this morning."

"I wish I had stock in FedEx."

"She said that you'd be here, and I was supposed to tell you these words: 'neon hand.' "

Neon hand. That was a clue. Ah, she had used this guy to deliver a clue and to test me, see if I'd rat her out. That hurt.

"Does that mean anything to you?" he said.

"Yeah, it's what you find in a fortune-teller's window."

"Does this mean anything?" he said, handing me a tear sheet.

It was from a local sex newspaper, dated 1983, which showed an ad for an escort service. Male escorts. I couldn't figure out what the hell this was about, until I looked a little more closely at the black-and-white picture in the ad, which showed four handsome men. One of them was Gabriel, the guy George had fixed me up with on our last night in New York, at the end of our week of dining, dancing, and getting free stuff from fashion designers. Gabriel wasn't an important character in the trip for me at all. We didn't hit it off. I didn't hit it off with any of the guys George had brought along when we all went out together.

Now that I thought about it, Gabriel forgot George's name a couple of times, and George paid for everything.

George had bought me a date.

This was the kind of thing Julie would have thought funny, but I just felt humiliated. Oddly enough, I've never had that much trouble getting dates on my own. But I guess it's a little harder to set someone up with a girl from out of town, sight unseen, who won't put out because she's being faithful to her asshole back-home boyfriend.

I looked at the guy sitting next to me with even more suspicion now. For all I knew, he was a male escort. That would play on Julie's sense of irony, to hire a male escort to deliver news about a male escort. Maybe he used that fake badge in his work for customers with a law-enforcement fetish—Hello, boy store? Send over a nice clean-cut-looking young man with handcuffs and a badge.

"What's the significance of this clipping?" asked "Special Agent" Walter.

"It's all just part of Julie's joke," I said.

"You sure you don't know where she is?"

"As I said, I haven't spoken to the woman since 1979. Are you sure you don't know where she is?" I asked, wiggling my eyebrows.

"Have you been drinking?" he asked.

"Two sips of a wine spritzer."

"Do you know Johnny Chiesa?" he asked in a whisper.

"Who the . . ." I began, and then stopped. No, I wasn't going to fall into this one. "Never heard of him."

"Special Agent" Walter gave me his card. "If you hear from her, call me. It's very important."

"Oh, sure," I said, paying the bartender and leaving. Yeah, wouldn't Julie love that, if I called up the FBI and asked for a nonexistent FBI agent. Or maybe there really was an agent by that name, who would listen to me and not have a clue what the hell I was talking about.

For a fleeting second, as I walked somewhat aimlessly towards the Bowery, I wondered if maybe that fed really was a fed. He was humorless enough to qualify.

"And a gang of wig-wearing women in Groucho-nose glasses are holding my intern Kathy hostage in order to get their granny back. Oh, right, Robin!" I said to myself, possibly aloud. "You're as bad as that guy leaning in the doorway there in the tinfoil earmuffs, cocking his head from side to side, humming, with a dazed look in his eyes."

"Moody's my friend," he said. "I came to see Moody."

He hummed some more, put his hands on his earmuffs like he was turning the dials on his head, and said, "Shadow Traffic."

"I'm probably crazier than he is." Then I realized I was talking to myself and shut my mouth.

Maybe the tinfoil guy wasn't nuts. Maybe he was just ahead of the curve. There used to be this guy who stood in front of the Jackson Broadcasting System building shouting about how our signals were frying his brain. Now, we know that people who live too close to transmission towers and big satellite dishes have a higher risk of brain cancer. And you've heard about people picking up radio signals in their fillings. So who knows. Maybe this guy was just one walking high-fidelity unit, trying to tune in a clear signal amidst all the static. Going from static to a faint country-Western signal to a news station to static to a taxi-cab dispatcher talking in rapid Hindi to a radio preacher whom he mistakes for the voice of God. I hoped he got an easy-listening station soon. Five gets you ten he had serious cooties when he was a kid.

Neon hand. That rang a bell in the back of my head. Or maybe it was the sound of my phone ringing again.

"Very good," said the voice on the phone. It was the head woman from the Groucho-nose-glasses gang. "You did very well. You passed the test."

And she hung up.

"Well, goody for me," I said. How did she know that guy had . . . Well, of course. They were all in cahoots with Julie and she'd set it all up. Duh.

Unfortunately, this clue wasn't going to do me much good. After Cafe Buñuel, I remembered, George and his friends had taken us back to our hotel, and along the way we made a couple of stops. While we were at a red light, Julie had caught the eye of a fortune-teller who was just about to turn off the giant neon hand in her window. She waved us in and on a lark we went, while George and his friends parked and patiently waited outside for us. It was irresistible, a real New York gypsy fortune-teller, with a big, heavy crucifix around her neck and a babushka scarf around her head, just like in the movies.

For five bucks, she read my palm and told me I'd be a television reporter. Lucky guess, right? Actually she whee-dled it out of me, though I didn't realize it at the time. Being a *tad* naïve, I thought she was gifted, but she just baited the hook and reeled me in. "I see you with a long stick of some kind," she said at one point. I responded, "A microphone?" "Yes, yes, a microphone. You're per-forming or . . ." "Reporting?" "Reporting, yes, you're a reporter, and I see you in a place with lot of grand old buildings. . . ." "Washington?" "Washington, yes."

The old gypsy told Julie she was going to be a great painter. Probably used the stick line on her too. A lot of people use sticks in their work, but if I hadn't responded to the stick, she could have kept prodding until some imagery connected with my secret dream. I'd seen Sally do this with people. Now that I was older and wiser, etc., I knew the tricks.

So, yeah, I knew where we'd gone next. But, damn, I'd never find that fortune-teller in this city, which has thousands of them. She was pretty old then. She was probably dead by now.

9

THE PHONE RANG AGAIN. Jeez, I was turning into one of those jerks who walk around talking on their cell phones all the time. I have a love-hate relationship with the telephone and have mixed feelings about people being able to reach me any time of the day or night no matter where I am.

"What now?" I said.

"Robin?"

"Claire! I'm so happy it's you!"

"I'm through. Where are you?"

"On Canal, heading towards the Bowery."

"Where can I meet you guys?"

"Singular. Tamayo got swept away by the Halloween Parade. Hmmm. You know the No-Name Diner on the Bowery, around Great Jones Street?"

"You know I hate burger joints."

"I'm tired and hungry and I have to have some red meat. I haven't eaten in a couple of hours. . . . So much stuff has happened. . . ."

After I gave her the headlines, she said, "Some friend, fucking up your night like this. Are you sure there's a reconciliation waiting for you at the end of this and not a confrontation?"

"You have to know Julie," I said. "And her sense of humor. I'll fill you in later."

"Okay. I'll meet you at the No-Name and bring the stuff I pulled for you. I just have to pick it up from the library."

"Do you have a costume? Because I'm in costume and if I look like a dork you have to look like a dork too."

"I checked out something from JBS props and costumes. I'll change into it. . . ."

"Please. And do me another favor. . . ."

"Okay."

"Do you still have the spare key to my place?"

"Yes."

"Can you stop at my place and bring me something?"

"Yeah, sure," she said. "What do you want?"

"It's a gold Godiva chocolate box in the bottom of my trunk at the end of my bed."

"Okay," she said.

"You're a pal. You sound blue. Are you okay?"

"Madri Michaels has read Solange's manuscript and she told me that I'm chapter fifteen."

"I heard."

"It's the second time in as many days Solange has directly or indirectly . . . Why do I care what she thinks? It's just, I have a few doubts myself still. . . ."

"I know you do."

"But I just couldn't see myself being a Washington political wife, you know? Dealing with all the reporters and the backstabbing, not to mention the asskissing."

"I know."

"Everything you do or say is completely picked apart and/or twisted."

"I know."

"Oh God. Did I do the right thing? Jess wasn't always so intransigent, you know. I was in love with him. He's going to be a great, great man and . . ."

In five minutes, if Claire continued this line of thought, I knew she would completely reverse herself, and be cursing her job and her own selfish dreams for taking her away from Jess, a good guy whom she had loved once, until you

were convinced she wanted to go back to him. But if you
suggested this, she'd reverse herself again, and end up crying. It was tiring, having to be so supportive on both sides
of an argument.

"My career is important. I couldn't be a reporter *and* a
political wife. At first it was okay, it was a new world, Jess
was great. . . ."

"It's okay, Claire. There, there . . ."

"Robin, don't do that," Claire said.

"Do what?"

"Be so . . . sympathetic, so. . . ."

"Nurturing."

"Yeah. If I want sympathy I'll call my grandma or my
sister."

"Well, what do you want from me, then?"

"I don't know. The usual. It's like the . . . Okay, you
know that diplomatic dinner I went to? The disaster? After
I pound my fist to make a point, sending my salad fork
somersaulting through the air towards an unsuspecting
waiter, I'd much rather have you or Tamayo say, 'You
nailed him! Good shot!' than have an oh-so-diplomatic
wife pat my shoulder and whisper—discreetly, for heaven's
sake—'That's okay. We'll get you another fork.' Then re-
sume discussing the business at hand."

"I think I know what . . ."

"She was trying to be kind, but I felt more embarrassed,
more awful. Do you understand?"

"Yeah."

I'd rather be loudly embarrassed and get a laugh out of
it, than quietly embarrassed by someone who is too well
meaning, though I'd rather not be embarrassed at all, and
I am much more of an expert on this subject than Claire,
for whom a flying fork is a once-in-a-lifetime experience.

Claire, for example, has never risen to accept an award, tripped over the hem of her dress, and accidentally pushed the mayor's face into his soup.

"When people feel sorry for me . . ."

"I dig, Claire."

"I'll see you in, say, a half-hour," she said, sounding irritated.

Boy, was she touchy these days. But she was going through a hard time, so I had to cut her some slack.

I wasn't always so extra-sensitive. You know, when I first heard about Claire's troubles that summer, the first thing I felt was a little schadenfreude rush. I hate to admit it, but I felt a bit relieved. I didn't want to feel that way, because she's a terrific person who got where she is by sheer force of will and talent and I love her blah blah blah, but there you go, that's the first thing I felt. I couldn't help it. Her life looked so perfect, and knowing it wasn't and she wasn't made me feel just a tad less inadequate next to her. One of the reasons I felt so inadequate next to her was racial. She had to overcome sexism *and* racism, whereas I only had to overcome one big external obstacle, and yet I hadn't done nearly as well as she had. That meant . . . omigod . . . some of my career problems had to come from . . . me, perhaps a few more than I had originally estimated. Not only that, but she had been doing very well in areas of failure for me. She's been a star Washington correspondent, a job I had tried and blown. Until it went kerblooey, she had been in a seemingly perfect love affair with one of the most eligible men in America.

After I got over that first thrill of shameful joy, my empathy kicked in, so much so that hearing her miserable made me miserable too. It also shook my confidence, because, if someone as supremely confident as Claire could get shaken like this, what hope did a neurotic like me have?

Even though she was younger than me, Claire, I realized, had become one of my role models—in some ways, not all. I'd learned a lot about confidence from her.

(I also learned a lot about national politics, synthetic languages, exotic diseases, and rural Southern folk magic. Her mother wrote quasi-anthropological books about folk magic, some of which was pretty wild. For instance, if you want to keep a man faithful, cook a little of your menstrual blood into his food. Eeuw. As Tamayo said, it may not keep a guy faithful, but just mention it and he'll think twice before he asks you to fetch his dinner.)

Long story short, what I learned was, schadenfreude aside, it's better to have happy, successful friends, because unhappy friends are a lot more grief. Plus, it's easier to borrow money from happy, successful friends, should the need arise.

How much the whole Jess thing tore Claire up became clear to me when I went to visit her in Washington, just after it all happened, and we rented *Casablanca*. Claire took *Casablanca* very personally. Did she defy her own nature and stay with Jess for the good of the nation, like Ingrid Bergman? Or did she choose television news, which would be the Humphrey Bogart character in this scenario? Or was it the other way around, was it better for the nation if she was a reporter and Jess was Humphrey Bogart? What about her needs? But it wasn't just *Casablanca*, it was shots of happy couples on television, even TV commercials in which supportive wives did laundry, cooked, or otherwise fussed over husbands and kids. Everything she watched, heard, saw seemed fraught with meaning for her, pricking a different question in her head.

In this state, she was especially vulnerable to Solange, who knew it and exploited it. What Solange had to gain from it, I'm not sure. There was no professional advantage—Solange had her own huge show and Claire was in General News. Maybe Solange was still trying to attract attention away from her own near-scandal the previous year, when it was discovered that her best-selling self-help affirmation tapes were being manufactured by slave laborers in drafty Chinese prisons. (Operations were quickly switched to a factory in Malaysia where they only exploited law-abiding grownups.)

The No-Name burger joint is a brightly lit and clean yet somehow dingy lunch counter where the customers look like the cast of *Barfly* and the staff all look like Lon Chaney. And they're not in costume. But the burgers are great and it's open twenty-four hours. I ordered one, along with a Coke, from the limping one-eyed waiter. He brought me a Diet Coke. Yuck. But rather than make him limp back to the end of the counter to replace it, I just poured a teaspoon of real sugar into it. Not being on the air anymore meant I could eat as much as I wanted and not worry about my weight. (The weird thing is, when I was on the air and worried about my weight, I was actually a little heavier.)

While I waited for my delicious, greasy, undercooked burger, I called home to see if any more occasional boyfriends were planning to drop in on me this weekend and join the orgy. There was a message from my mother: "I had another lovely talk with your friend Sally this week while you were away. What a highly intelligent young woman."

Though I didn't approve of my friends' consulting Sally, I thought it was kind of sweet, my mom and Sally becoming friends. Sally's mom was dead, and it seemed like, well, good karma that she could enjoy my mom. It wasn't like Sally could make my mom any nuttier than she already was, or vice versa.

My mom is nutty like a genius, and in a benevolent way.

Sally has this theory about my mother, who believes she is a member of the British royal family. Sally believes my mother *was* a member of the British royal family—in a past life—and her past life and this life are just more mixed up together than is normal.

"I'm a bit worried about Sally, though. Did you know that experimental medication she is taking has caused a numbness in her left arm?" my mother said, and urged me to check up on Sally.

Now I had to worry about Sally's left arm too, on top of everything else. I was rapidly approaching Worry Overload. Sally had been working as a human guinea pig since she found herself having a crisis of faith and on the verge of bankruptcy. "Cosmically," one day she was scanning the back-page classifieds of *The Village Voice* "looking for a sign" when she saw that a local medical center was offering to pay people to participate in an eczema study. Having eczema was a prerequisite, and Sally didn't have eczema or know how to acquire it, but the ad started her thinking. Turns out you can make decent money being a human guinea pig if you're willing to take pills and sign a legal waiver. She was able to make $400 a week in a three-month study of headache medication, and was now getting $1,000 a week in a PMS-pill study. She said she figured it was her moral duty, and a good karma-clearer, to offer herself up and spare some poor lab rat the possible side effects: mood swings and weight gain. Lord knows, New York doesn't need any more overweight, manic-depressive rodents.

"Don't forget Sally's birthday is coming up," my mother concluded. "And don't forget to call home on Sunday."

I hadn't forgotten Sally's birthday, although finding a present was tricky. While in L.A., I'd gone looking for a present for her on Melrose.

"May I help you?" a young woman asked me, flashing

a banal smile. I told her I needed a present for a girlfriend.

"What kind of woman is she?" asked the clerk. The question struck me as so bizarre. Did she really want to know? I knew what the clerk expected me to say, that Sally's tall, about thirty years old, an Ivy Leaguer, favorite color is blue, that kind of thing. But I decided to tell her exactly what Sally was like. "Well," I said, "she's a bald witch with a degree in comparative religion from Princeton who can't keep a boyfriend, and in a previous life she was a murderous Sumerian harlot."

"Oh," the clerk said, not missing a beat. "Perhaps a scarf?"

The limping one-eyed waiter brought my burger, and as I raised it to my mouth I caught my reflection in the window. My hair was even worse now. Now I looked like a redheaded albino Buckwheat. I had a lot of nerve criticizing Sally's looks.

Then my reflection dissolved, and I saw past it to a disheveled guy outside, who was riding a bike in a semi-circle on the sidewalk. It was almost eleven, according to the Marlboro Lights clock on the wall of the diner, and he was riding a bike on the Bowery. What a nut. He looked like he was wearing yellow crime-scene tape as a bandanna, but when he got closer I saw that the yellow plastic tape, unevenly torn and unevenly tied around his stringy-haired head, said "Caution—Radioactive." He was singing, loudly, over and over, "Country roads, take me home, to the place I belong," while people dodged his shaky bicycle.

The microchip in my buttocks was beeping like crazy, and I fugued.

⚙ 10 ⚙

I READ SOMEWHERE that most people's vision of the future is really just their idealized vision of the past, and I guess that's true, because sometimes, when my job, my love life, and the big city seem too fucking complicated, I close my eyes to daydream and see this golden image of Ferrous on a childhood summer day, the smell of lawn, grape Kool-Aid, and charcoal briquets in the air, Julie Goomey and me on the porch, and Doug Gribetz riding his Stingray bicycle back and forth in front of my house.

Ferrous was a company town which, along with four neighboring towns, made up Five Towns County. Long after the iron-skillet factory finally closed for good in 1983, we had a sign at the town limits that showed a smiling, 1950s housewife holding a skillet with eggs and bacon in it. "Ferrous, Minnesota, Iron Skillet Capital of the World," the sign said. Underneath in smaller letters was the phrase "Home of the Fanning Even-Flo Skillet."

Sixty years or so earlier, Mrs. Gerda Fanning had complained about food sticking in her skillet for the umpteenth time, and her husband, Tikki "Tom" Fanning, the owner of a small foundry that processed iron ore into bars, got an idea. What if there was a layer of air between two layers of cast iron? For months he experimented, until he came up with a skillet that worked the way he wanted, reducing stick and cooking food more evenly. This was a huge leap forward in skillet technology, at least that's what the tour guide on the school field trip always said. And there would be more great leaps—carbon cores, grease-catcher troughs, preseasoned finishes, etc. etc.—before labor difficulties, Teflon, Pyrex, and foreign competition took away huge chunks of Fanning's business, leading to its ultimate demise.

The sign survived for years, until Vision 21 Consolidated Industries moved its headquarters to Ferrous and began manufacturing new things, most notably the Zipper Sit-Down Scooter. You know, those motorized half-scooter/half-shopping-cart contraptions that are taking over the Sun Belt.

That's where we came from, me and Julie. It was a sweet-smelling place a hundred miles south of the Canadian border, where people tried to keep their secrets, and the town was ruled by two families, the Fannings, who owned the ironworks, and the MacCoshams, who owned almost everything else.

But if I daydream about it too long, the sunny image sometimes dissolves into another, less sunny one.

The first time I heard Julie Goomey's name was just before Christmas in fifth grade, when Mrs. Oatwig, our teacher, told us we were going to have a new classmate the next day, Julie Goomey, who had just moved here, and whose father had died the year before in Vietnam. At recess, Mary MacCosham and Sis Fanning said they'd seen the new girl, and filled the schoolyard in on what they "knew" about her. The new girl looked like Lily Munster with glasses, Mary said, dubbing her Goony Goomey and declaring her to have cooties. According to Mary, Julie's mom was a tramp and a drunk, and her dad had been killed running from a battle.

When Julie appeared in class with long dark hair and very white skin, Mary MacCosham's Lily Munster imagery was fresh in our minds, and everyone started laughing. I admit I did too. I admit also that my first instinct on hearing about Julie was, maybe this is someone next to whom I'll look great in contrast. Maybe she would replace me as a cootie girl and I could get promoted from outcast to neutral kid, or even toady to the cool kids.

Mrs. Oatwig chewed out the class for laughing, which did nothing to raise Julie's stock. Any girl who got the whole class in trouble earned a fistfight after school with Herbie Hofstetler, who only liked to fight girls, preferably his own height or shorter.

Julie just stood there in front of the class, her white skin now burning red, her eyes shut, her jaw clenched, as if not seeing us would make us all go away. That's when I started feeling bad for her. She was a fatherless cootie girl, and my empathy kicked in.

A couple of the neutral girls stopped after class very discreetly and kindly to say hello to Julie, but there was no move to actually befriend her. After they left and nobody was looking, I invited Julie to come over and hang out in my clubhouse, which was really a bomb shelter my father had put in the back yard just after the Cuban Missile Crisis.

But, you know, she rebuffed me. Funny, I'd forgotten all about that, how Julie didn't want to be my friend at first. She wanted to be Mary MacCosham's friend, for chrissake, and set about trying to ingratiate herself to Mary in the subsequent weeks. Mary, oh so amused by it all, privately invited Julie to her Christmas Tea, and when Julie asked her, in front of other girls, what she should wear, Mary laughed and loudly denied ever inviting Julie.

"Who'd invite you to a Christmas Tea?" Mary said. "Maybe a Cootie Tea." Mary MacCosham, class wit.

God, I felt so bad for Julie, because Mary had pulled the same stunt with me a year before, when she privately invited me to her Spring Strawberry Tea. (Mary and her coterie were big on having teas, at which soft drinks were served but never tea. They were pretentious that way.)

When I told my mother about Julie, she called Julie's

mother to invite Julie to my place for our own Tea. Mom also invited the other cootie girl, Mabel. So I guess we did have a Cootie Tea. That's when Julie and I hit it off, discovering all the things we had in common, including a morbid infatuation with the late Robert F. Kennedy and a passion for pirate movies. Neither of us clicked with poor Mabel, who only wanted to play dolls, which Julie and I weren't into by fifth grade. Mabel, poor Mabel. We pretty much ignored her. She didn't even have another cootie girl to play with, just her beloved dolls. Though Mabel and I were outcasts, once Julie arrived it was she who bore the brunt of Mary and Sis's tortures.

With the exception of a few cool teachers, the grownups thought Mary and Sis were angels, because Mary and Sis acted like angels in front of the grownups, and it was dangerous to rat them out to the grownups in our town. If you got Mary and Sis in any trouble, you earned yourself a whole lot more trouble. Mabel told her mother that Mary was torturing her at recess, and Mabel's mother, a large divorced woman with BO and very hairy arms who worked as a cleaning woman at the ironworks, complained to Mary's mother. Not long after that, Mary and Sis and a few of their toadies ambushed Mabel after school and took her to Sis's house, where they played kangaroo court with her, tried her for crimes against them, the ruling elite, and as punishment made her drink a concoction made up of various condiments and pieces of Mabel's favorite Barbie doll, which they had tried to puree in a blender. If Mabel ratted them out again, they warned, her mother would be fired.

Or so the playground rumor went. It didn't help that most of our parents worked for either the MacCoshams or the Fannings and that Mary and Sis reminded us of this frequently. Neither of my parents had worked for them, and neither did Julie's mom. Though we were pretty poor, they had no economic power over us. Hmmm. Now that I'm older and wiser, etc., I wonder if this wasn't one of the things that ticked Sis and Mary off about me and Julie, and made them find a different kind of power, the power of the cootie.

Cooties, jeez. I hadn't thought about cooties for ages. Water under the bridge. I was a long way from fifth grade. So why did I think to myself, "As soon as I have some free time, I am going to go to Mary MacCosham's, wait outside her fancy Upper East Side apartment building, and then punch her right in her carefully doctored nose"?

On second thought, that would probably be overkill, because we got more or less even with Mary the summer before we went to high school. Among other things we did to harass her, we sent her name in as a sales lead to a bunch of industrial-trash-can companies, and a succession of salesmen of faux Dumpsters showed up on her doorstep. That one was my idea. Julie, of course, went me one better when we worked at the MacCosham-owned Camp Hapalot.

By this time, Mary's tactics had improved. She knew she could silence Julie, me, or just about anyone else she wanted to with a few choice words. Now I know these to be control words. All Mary had to say to shut me up was, "How's your mother the queen?," and because I didn't necessarily want to tell cute guy counselors from as far away as Canada and Chicago that my mother believed she was the rightful queen of England, I would just shut up and let Mary inflict all sorts of slights and insults on me.

Now I know that these control words work only if you let them work, so you have some control over them.

With Julie, Mary would talk about drunks, or cowardice in battle, or, even more nakedly, call her Garage Goomey, the nickname Julie graduated to in junior high, when she suddenly sprouted tits. The boys said she'd do it with anyone in her garage for a quarter. It wasn't true, but nobody cared. I mean, they all chose to believe the worst about her, and me. The joke went that Garage Goomey would do it for a quarter, Hudson would pay the boys a quarter. Har-har.

(The Hofstetler kid, who only fought girls his own height or shorter, started the Garage thing. I'd have to remember to put him on my punch-in-the-nose list, show up on his doorstep one day, say, "This is what you get for beating on girls, you shithead," and then pop him right in the kisser.)

While Julie and I worked at Camp Hapalot, in the kitchen and sanitation respectively, for the money and the chance to meet college boys from exotic places like Chicago and Canada, Mary MacCosham worked as a full-fledged counselor, and went a different route, boy-wise.

The first thing Julie noticed after we arrived was that Virgin Mary had packed an awful lot of Intimate Secrets Deodorant, a feminine-hygiene spray to make one's genitalia smell like an English country garden. As Julie figured it, nobody needed that much vaginal deodorant unless she was expecting someone else to do a lot of sniffing down there.

Julie was a damn good spy, better than Harriet the Spy, in part because she suffered from hyperaccusis, which is hyperactive hearing. (All the women in Julie's family had it, and in her mother it eventually turned to objective tinnitus. Tinnitus is when you hear a ringing in your ears. Objective tinnitus is when other people hear the ringing in your ears.)

When Julie heard Mary sneaking out of the bunkhouse in the middle of the night, she followed, as quiet as an

Iroquois, and discovered that Mary was making the beast with two backs in the chapel with Leonard, a handsome guy who worked in the stables. It was so Chatterley.

What I would have done with this information was go to Mary and say, "Look, I know about you and Leonard and I don't think your family, especially your mother, would be too thrilled. So lay off me and Julie."

But Julie was so much better at this. She said nothing. Instead, she left little notes around Mary's bunk. Because Julie's handwriting always gave her away, she asked me to type the notes for her on my portable typewriter. The first said, "The little chapel?" followed by a note saying, "Leonard," and finally, simply, "I'm watching you."

After that, Mary was pretty subdued around us. Getting Mary, and good, put the wind in Julie's sails, and took it out of Mary's. Mary started fucking up a bit, and Julie became more confident than I'd ever seen her.

Knowing Mary was boffing the horse guy in the chapel makes me think more kindly of her now. The sexual revolution hadn't really hit Ferrous by then, where it was the 1950s until the 1970s and then it was 1962 for about five years. Being older and wiser, etc., I now suspect everyone was having sex of some kind and pretending they weren't. If they weren't having sex, they wanted to awful badly.

If Mary's ex-husband could be believed, she had a thing for working-class guys, though it didn't come out in the open until after her mother died.

Mary's mother—eee-yai—rats up both trouser legs. What a scary woman, in an unkindly kind way. When I was a kid, if she saw me in the street, she'd inquire, "Hello, dear, how is your poor mother? You poor, poor dears. Wouldn't you like her to go to the hospital in Newton, get some rest?" Yeah, sure, what kid doesn't want her mother carted off to the hospital in Newton, or, as it was also known, Nuttown, because it was home to the county psychiatric facility (now a major drug-and-alcohol rehab center).

Mrs. MacCosham was Mrs. Perfect, and it upset her greatly that there were any unruly people living in her town, marring her vision of things. Now, older and wiser, etc., I know that she was nuts too.

Oddly enough, Julie and Mary later became friends for a while. Shortly before Julie and I had our falling-out in July 1979, Mary had a huge falling-out with Sis Fanning. It must have been going around, like a virus, or maybe it was just that we were all at a particular crossroads in our lives, moving from minority to legal adulthood, casting off some things and taking up others, etc. But though Sis and I didn't hit it off, Julie and Mary, united by their mutual hatred of me and Sis, became fast friends during my last summer in Ferrous. Mary and Julie even took a four-day shopping trip to New York in the late summer. But they too had a falling-out soon afterwards.

Mary's mother hated me, but she hated Julie even more. Probably that played a part in Julie and Mary's brief friendship, that Mary was rebelling against her mother, taking a walk on the wild side with Julie.

Here in Gotham, Mary wasn't one of the cool kids. Even before her motherfucker of a midlife crisis, she was in a social rut, unable to advance to the upper echelons with Ivana and Blaine and disenfranchised European princesses from countries no longer on the map. She was like a toady to the cool kids, or the ones she thought were cool anyway. That had to be frustrating for someone who had grown up being the most popular. Or the most powerful. I sometimes get those two confused.

Every now and then, I saw Mary in the New York social columns, you know, a minor boldface mention here and there, one name in a long list of names of people who put together the annual gala to benefit the peasants, that kind of thing. The pictures I'd seen of her in the social columns were kind of sad. It always looked like the photographer was taking a picture of someone else and Mary had jumped into the background.

A LARGE DOG came up and sat down next to me at the lunch counter.

"Howdy, Miss Robin," she said. That Southern "Miss Robin" thing threw me for a second. I thought it was Kathy. But she was too tall and the voice was too deep.

"Claire, that's your costume? Jojo the Health and Safety Dog?"

"Cute, ain't it?"

To help satisfy the FCC rule on educational programming for children, one of ANN's sister networks did kids' news cut-ins during the Saturday-morning cartoons. The late-morning cut-ins were anchored by regular kids in the seven-to-twelve-year-old range, but the early cut-ins were anchored by people in animal costumes, and were designed to explain current events to three-year-olds. So, for example, Anchor Bear would read a story about the Middle Eastern peace process, Anchor Poodle would talk about the unemployment figures, and then they'd throw to Jojo the Health and Safety Dog in the field for a story about playground safety. I shouldn't laugh. Their ratings were a little better than the grownup news on ANN at the same time, and their demographics—impressionable, spoiled, and affluent youngsters—were far more appealing to advertisers.

"Why did you pick that costume?"

"I just grabbed something from JBS props and costumes when I was at work. It was either this, Anchor Bear, or Washington Walrus."

Claire was in New York to fill in on the anchor desk for Sawyer Lash, who was on parental leave looking after his new baby.

She took the head off and kissed my cheek. "It's good to see you. What are you supposed to be?"

"A freshly undead person. See the bat biting my neck? But thanks to my frizzy hair I look more like an electrocution victim, I know."

"Did you bring the Godiva box?" I asked.

She kept talking over my question. These days, she needed to talk about herself a lot, and she's a *tad* self-absorbed at the best of times. But since I had often bent her ear with my problems, it was the least I could do to do the good-friend thing and put her needs ahead of mine for a spell.

"I was going to wear a glamorous costume, then I thought, Why not be goofy for a change? I need more fun. The costume has to be back in props by 4:30 A.M. or else Dr. Solange Stevenson is in trouble," Claire said.

"Why Solange?"

"I signed it out in her name," Claire said.

"A prank? That isn't like you."

"As I told you, I'm pissed at Solange, and not just because of her damned book. Yesterday, her new flunky producer called me up to see if I'd take part in a show about the children of mixed-race unions called 'Black on the Outside, White on the Inside.' "

"You should do what Louis Levin does. Whenever he runs into Solange, he just calls her 'massuh,' and that shuts her right up," I said. "You know, because of the slave labor in the Chinese prisons."

"I'm not white on the inside, whatever the hell that means," Claire snapped. "I'm half African-American, through and through, and I'm proud of it. I'm not going to say 'massuh' to some white woman with an impacted colon, even as a joke. Slavery isn't funny."

"Jeez. Okay, then. Call Susan Brave, get some other dirt on her."

"I'm not going to stoop to Solange's level."

"Well, do what Tamayo does. When Solange says anything to you, just think, 'I'm rubber, you're glue, whatever you say bounces off me and sticks to you.'"

"Thank you," she said sarcastically.

"I . . ." I began, and stopped, not sure what to say, since I couldn't seem to say anything to her tonight without touching a nerve. I've been there yadda yadda yadda, but it still felt lousy to get snapped at when my intentions were good. I didn't know how to make her feel better. If I was too nurturing, she snapped at me; if I suggested she get into therapy to help her with her compulsive spending, she accused me of meddling and assured me she could afford to be a spendthrift. If I tried to reassure her, she jumped down my throat. Laughing one minute, snapping or bursting into tears the next—these tricky emotional waters of hers were hard to navigate.

"I'm dreading this book coming out, even if she has *thinly* disguised me as an African-American actress who ditched a prominent black philanthropist in favor of doing a T&A sitcom. Everyone who has read it so far knew it was me," Claire said. "On the other hand, Tamayo's proud of being in her book. Free publicity, she says." Thinking about Tamayo made her laugh. "Oh, forget about Solange. Fuck Solange," she said.

"You're cussing a lot lately."

"It's from hanging out with bad companions," she said, and smiled at me. "Speaking of which, Tamayo called me while I was on my way to your place. She's at a party in the Flatiron District with three of the 52 Sons of Ramses, whatever the hell that means."

"How come she called you and not me?"

"She couldn't remember your cell-phone number."

"But she remembers yours?"

"You've been out of town, so she's called mine more often lately. You know how she is about things like phone numbers and birthdays. She never remembers those things."

"Did you give her my number?"

"She would have just forgotten it. But I got the address for the party. I thought we could swing by and get her. I could use some of that Tamayo magic tonight."

"Did you get the stuff I asked for?"

"Yeah," she said, whipping out her Reporter's Notebook. "This is what the library found on Julie Goomey, which is old. She had one phone number and one address from 1985 to 1990, and it was in New York City, on York Avenue in the upper 80s."

Boy, that hit me hard, that we'd lived in the same city for so many years and she'd never tried to contact me before now.

What happened to her after 1990?

"There was a mention of her in *Fortune* magazine in 1988 as a rising young star in the international-finance division of Peyser & Peyser, and then another mention in *Business Week* in 1990, when she was fired because of some account irregularities. Then nothing. She vanished from New York.

"The library also checked out Help for Kids. The office is on Park Avenue in the 60s. It's a nonprofit corporation, as opposed to a charitable organization. I'm not clear on the distinction there, but I think it has something to do with less stringent regulations."

"They can't make a profit, but they aren't required to give away money. Something like that," I said.

"It's about six months old and its main work is distributing money to other charities. The members of the board are all low-grade prominent people and their involvement seems to be largely honorary, you know, something nice for an executive who's thinking of running for City Council to have on his résumé."

"Headed by Anne Winston."

"Right. There are a zillion Winstons in the directory—I couldn't find anything more. New York State offices are closed."

"And my Godiva box?"

"Oh yeah." She dug in her leather backpack and pushed it across the counter at me and ordered a coffee. A regular coffee. Drinking coffee, cussing, spending, playing pranks, being goofy. She was going to hell in a handbasket.

The Godiva box was kind of crushed, and the gilt had worn off the edges. Almost reverentially, I opened it. I hadn't looked at this stuff in probably ten years. In it was a stack of square snapshots with white borders, a bunch of matchbooks, ticket stubs, swizzle sticks, cocktail napkins, an old subway token, a Macy's receipt, etc.

Claire still had a lot she needed to talk about, so I listened to her with half my brain, while studying my souvenirs with the other half, trying to balance her immediate need to talk with mine to figure out where to go next. I went through all the mementos, looking for something that would help me decipher the neon-hand clue, since I hadn't a hope in hell of finding that old fortune-teller.

The problem was, I remembered going to all these places, but I didn't always remember when or with whom I'd gone to them. A MOMA pin—I was fairly certain I'd gone there one afternoon with Julie, just Julie. A Macy's receipt, with Julie. Cocktail napkins from the Sirocco Club, the Rainbow Room, and the Brass Rail, a matchbook from Jimmy Ryan's jazz joint, swizzle sticks from various discos—all places I'd gone with George, Julie, and one or another of his unmemorable friends. Maybe it was a place without mementos, though we'd managed to find some scrap of something in most of the places we'd gone.

". . . and I think I said something stupid to Matt Dillon after our interview segment," Claire said.

"What? Matt Dillon? What did you say to him?"

"I don't remember! I was so . . . Two or three nights ago, I had this very erotic dream involving Matt Dillon on a dark field full of glowing white weather balloons. It is unnerving to meet someone you've recently had a sex dream about."

"I doubt you said anything stupid. . . ."

"Robin, please don't do that."

"Do what?"

"Whatever you're doing."

"I'm not being sympathetic, I'm giving you my opinion. Jeez."

"You . . . just assume I didn't say anything stupid. . . . I don't know. I appreciate your faith in me, but I feel like I'm not living up to it right now and . . ." she stuttered.

"Well, sorry for whatever. Jesus."

"No, I'm sorry. It's all this shit. The Jess business, my thirtieth birthday is coming up, things have been going wrong for me lately, and I am having a hard time articulating how I feel."

"It's okay. . . . Oh, I don't mean to be sympathetic when I say it's okay. I just mean, fugedaboudit."

She smiled.

"Were you wearing that costume when you said something stupid to Matt Dillon?" I asked.

She laughed. "No. That would have been funny."

I didn't hear the rest of what she said. I'd reached the bottom of the Godiva box, and found the other half of the dollar bill.

"de me tuer," it said in French. To kill me.

I had to check it twice, put it together with the first part of the dollar to make sure the serial numbers matched. "Il essaie de me tuer." There was no mistake. The message George had written on the dollar bill was, He is trying . . . to kill me. What was it, some kind of joke?

"This is really bizarre," I said to Claire.

"You sure this is a PR stunt?"

"The charity checks out, right? But this seems tailor-made for me. And Kathy called from the charity's phone number. . . . It's weird—'He is trying to kill me.'"

"Maybe that was his joke, once he realized you didn't really speak French. His way of confirming that."

"A joke, like the one about me being an ironworks heiress. Yeah. 'He's killing me.' Like the way people come up to Tamayo after a show and tell her, You kill me. But that the dollar says this, and Julie set this up as a charity murder mystery—"

"She probably doesn't know what it says, seeing as you've had the half that referred to killing and haven't seen her in all these years."

"Yeah. It's probably just an amazing coincidence." I have a tendency to leap to extreme conclusions. Same thing happened when I started seeing Mike. Mike has a dark, Irish side, and the blood of twenty-seven kamikaze pariah dogs on his soul, all mowed down on the unlit back roads of the Northwest Frontier of Pakistan, and because of it, I pushed him away. Then my super, Phil, gave me some good advice. Don't turn this into one of your plots, Robin, he said. Just listen, and he'll reveal himself.

"But after the shit you've been through because of murders, you'd think she'd do something else, a scavenger hunt or something, if she wanted to play a good-natured joke and pull your nostalgia strings," Claire said.

"That wouldn't be Julie, to be good-natured and soft and squishy like that. She knew of my unhealthy interest in homicide, so she probably thought this would be a treat for me. I haven't seen her in a loooong time; maybe she isn't up on my unfortunate involvement in those two murder cases. Maybe she doesn't know that's all behind me now."

"How strange this is happening on a Girls' Night Out."

"Well, obviously, she didn't know about that," I said. "She planned this around Halloween."

"How did she know you'd be in town?"

"I don't know."

Claire's reporter instincts were kicking in. She was interviewing me.

"How did she know you'd follow the clues?"

"She knows my curiosity. We did this as kids, sent each other all over the place to pick up clues."

"What did you get at the end of the quest?"

"Candy, *Tiger Beat* magazines, that kind of thing when we were little. Jewelry, perfume, books, concert tickets when we were older. Or information sometimes. One time she sent me all the way to Duluth to a drugstore clerk to find the answer to the question: Who is Sis Fanning going to the Greaser Days Dance with? Sometimes it took me weeks to solve her puzzles, thanks to her false leads."

Claire had a light in her eyes.

"Let's approach this from a reporter's standpoint, not an unobjective old-friend standpoint," she said. "Kathy obviously did. She got to the charity office. That's got to be the last stop. Why don't we just go to the charity office, since Kathy called from there?"

"But I called there several times and no one was there. I got the answering machine, so I figured they went to wherever we were going to party later."

"All that means is that the answering machine was on. Your pal Julie wanted you to go through all this rigmarole, take you down memory lane, so she wasn't going to pick up on your voice."

"You could be right. But that sounds too easy for something Julie plotted. . . ."

"We go to the source, cut out all the steps in between, and find your old friend and your intern. You've been out of the field too long, Robin. You gotta get out from under that administrative crap you do and get back on a story. Let's go."

I hadn't seen a free cab all night, but Claire has this talent, among others—she can almost always get a cab.

"I think she's fucking with you, Robin," Claire said of Julie as we rode uptown to the Flatiron District to pick up Tamayo.

"Claire, you have to know Julie," I said. "A perverse sense of humor and love of a good girlish prank was something we shared. When I think of what she did to Mrs. Hobbins—or Old Hobnail, as we knew her—I still laugh, a little guiltily."

"Old Hobnail?"

"The sewing teacher from hell, a Waffen-SS type with Queen Elizabeth's wardrobe, back in seventh and eighth grades, when sewing and cooking classes (home ec) were still mandatory for girls at my school."

God, I hated sewing class. The machine scared me, with its razor-sharp needle going a hundred miles an hour. I was afraid I was going to accidentally stitch my thumb to a piece of stretch terry. But Julie was even worse at it than me. She was almost failing the course when we came to the Corduroy Unit of our sewing curriculum. A daunting material, corduroy, the Viet Cong of fashion fabric. It was to be her Dien Bien Phu.

After two weeks of fear, frustration, and tears, she finally turned in her corduroy project, only to have Mrs. Hobbins hold it up in class and ridicule it in front of our peers.

To be fair, her project was truly a disaster, a jumpsuit with twisted seams and one leg shorter than the other—as Hobbins pointed out, an outfit suitable only for a polio victim. But Julie hated Old Hobnail after that. The next class, before Hobnail got there, Julie discreetly poured water in the hollow of her wooden chair—just a little, so that she might not feel it through her bomb-grade corsetry, but enough that she'd look like she wet herself when she got up.

This is precisely what happened. When Hobnail turned to the blackboard and displayed her wet ass to the class, the loud laughter of the girls tipped her off that something was up. Strangely, though, she didn't accuse Julie. She accused me, and though I denied it, she kept me after class.

The next year, we were put in separate sewing classes, the theory being that separately we were inert substances, volatile only when mixed.

"Is this Julie worth all this trouble?" Claire asked.

"To me she is. Because of her, I moved to New York. And because of her, I became semipopular in high school, and redeemed my cooties somewhat."

"I can't wait to meet her," Claire said.

☼ **12** ☼

WE HAD TO PICK UP TAMAYO, so we went up to East 25th Street, just off Madison Square Park, site of the Rocking Chair Riots of 1901. When I first heard about those riots, I imagined a bunch of old people beating on cops with their rocking chairs. But actually the riots were started by a young guy who sat in a public rocking chair in Madison Square and refused to pay the nickel rental fee that the city charged.

The party was in a huge duplex with pillars holding up the ceiling and very little furniture. "Young, nasty hipsters," as Claire put it, and Wannabeats jammed the place, most standing but others sitting on everything, hanging off the steel-mesh staircase in the back, lounging on top of amps. The crowd was young, twentyish, likely single. Most were moshing, kind of bobbing up and down, because there wasn't enough room to dance. You could hardly breathe, and when you did you took in a lungful of cigarette and pot smoke.

(As I looked for Tamayo, I caught a whiff of cigarettes and strawberry perfume, mingled, and I had a midlife moment. For a second there, I was transported back to a dark rec room, necking with a boy whose bubble gum had formed a thin sugar crust on his lips, and suddenly in my head I heard Cher singing "Gypsies, Tramps and Thieves.")

Two mummies holding hands passed by, and I remembered that I had to make a decision about Mike or Eric. If it was going to be Eric, I should call Mike and just tell him to can the weekend and I'd see him in two weeks, when I had to go to Vegas for an affiliates meeting. Or maybe I should be responsible, and not see either of them, stay in and do work instead, since I had reports due Monday, etc. It wasn't like I was doing some huge favor for Eric or Mike by seeing them. Eric was reeaallly good-looking, and funny too, a good guy, and he could scare up companionship pretty easily. Mike wasn't such a hound, and if we couldn't get together when he was in town, he'd hang out with his daughter Samantha. . . .

Oh, hell, I thought. I'll worry about it later.

It was too noisy to have a conversation here; music from early-1960s spy shows was blasting away. The idea seemed to be to just bump randomly into other bodies all night until you bumped into one you liked and then leave with it. When I was younger, I loved scenes like this, but unless you're energetic and in full mating mode, what's the point of standing around in a noisy, smoky room for even five minutes?

It took more than five minutes to track down Tamayo, who was out on the fire escape talking about her UFO movie to a comic-book illustrator, not in costume, and a guy dressed like a Klingon.

"But if the two black holes are connected by a tunnel, or what is known as a wormhole, and the mouths of the black holes meet, as they would eventually, then the people on this planet would travel back to their own pasts," the Klingon said. "Maybe to their own futures."

"And how would that affect their weight?" Tamayo asked. "Would it fluctuate wildly?"

"I'm not sure they would weigh more in the first place. I don't know. I'm confused," the Klingon said.

I admired how Tamayo could get a man trying to hit on her into a conversation about quantum physics.

"Know how Klingons flirt?" Tamayo asked, when we finally dragged her out. "The Klingon word for 'love' is

bang, and the word for 'yes' is *HISlaH. Bang? HISlaH.*
That's an entire romantic interaction."

"Did that Klingon use that on you?" I said.

"Yeah."

"That explains why there are so few Klingons in the
world," I said.

"Where are we going?" Tamayo asked.

"Park and 62nd, to find Kathy and Julie. There have
been a few wrinkles since I lost you in the parade."

Claire filled Tamayo in on the key things, and also mentioned Solange's new book.

"So what do you care what Solange says? Remember
what you told me when I started doing stand-up full-time?
If you're going to swim with the sharks, don't wear a raw-
beef bathing suit. Good advice."

Claire said, "It's not what she thinks, it is what other
people will . . ."

"The swells will know she's full of shit. There isn't anything you can do about the squares except win them over
through your work. Otherwise ignore them. Did Robin tell
you how I offended Solange with an armpit fart at one of
those Womedia things?"

"No, I didn't," I said. "Why don't you tell her?"

Tamayo had the world broken down into swells and
squares. Swells, presumably, include those people who
laugh at quality fart jokes. Solange was not in this number,
as we discovered at a Womedia fund-raiser organized by
Solange and featuring a dance piece choreographed by a
guy Solange wanted to boink. I took Tamayo so I could
introduce her to some of my sweller Womedia sisters who
might be able to help her career. Solange did not appreciate
Tamayo's making fart noises, or, as Solange put it, "vulgar
noises," with her armpit during "sensitive parts of the
performance."

That sounds crude, I know, fart noises, but it was Tamayo's timing that made that work. See, the female dancer had her back to the male lead, and he was holding on to her, slowly sliding down her back to his knees, and when his face got to her butt, Tamayo did the fart thing. Childish, yes. Nobody but those people immediately around us heard the fart, but Solange heard it—and was not amused. Stifling hysterics, we had to leave.

Perhaps we shouldn't have had those preshow Rob Roys at Hojo's.

Not that we're completely uncultured boors—not all the time. But it was a shitty dance piece, called *X/Y*, tedious and pretentious, a couple in spandex essentially doing what we used to call dry-humping back at Hummer High School in Ferrous, Minnesota. I hasten to add that the *New York Times* dance critic also panned the piece, although she expressed herself somewhat more eloquently than Tamayo. In any event, some of my more serious Womedia sisters felt the armpit fart was inappropriate, and I could see their point of view too, you know.

Tamayo's retelling of this had Claire laughing her ass off, and Claire was suddenly fine again. They talked about people I didn't even know, nights they'd gone out together to interesting-sounding places, like Mugsy's Chow Chow and the Bubble Lounge, and exchanged information about all the new trendy places. They poked fun at each other and did that home-girl, hands-on-hips, side-to-side head-bob thing, which Tamayo, mimic extraordinaire, had taught to Claire. The circle of their intimacy drew a little tighter, and seemed to have a little less room for me.

It bothered me a little, I admit, how *my* friends and former producers Tamayo and Claire had become such good friends when I wasn't there. At first, I couldn't figure out what they had in common, but it turned out the mixed-race business gave them a lot of common ground. They were both former special-report producers, roughly the same age, late twenties, and closer in age to each other than to me. They both had, under normal conditions, an excess of self-confidence.

On the dissonant side, Claire was a vegetarian, whereas Tamayo was a carnivore and had eaten whale once, which she found a tad oily. She even had an Eat More Whale bumper sticker from an Eat More Whale campaign in Japan a few years back, though as a joke, not because she was for eating whales. Claire is very tolerant of people who eat meat, though she never gives up her campaign to get other people to give it up, but she was pretty rabid about some things, like saving the whales, and didn't have a good sense of humor about it. Still, despite this difference, she and Tamayo had bonded, leading me to wonder how I fit into this Benetton tableau vivant.

Tamayo read my mind. "Hey, look at us, we're like 'Charlie's Angels' for the nineties. A black chick, a Jap chick, and the token dead redhead. I forgot to tell you, Robin, we have a new security trick for you," Tamayo said. "It's an Elayne Boosler trick. You get six locks, and you lock three of them, so if a burglar tries to pick your locks he'll always be locking three and unlocking three."

"Isn't that a great idea?" Claire said. "When she told us . . ."

"*She* told you this?"

"Last night, at this party we went to. Boosler was there and Tamayo introduced me to her. We would have invited you along, but you were in L.A."

"I always miss these parties for some reason." I admit I am a tad starstruck and get a kick out of meeting celebrities. I'd love the chance to say something stupid to Matt

Dillon sometime. I guess that's the small-town girl in me.

"I was in L.A. having dinner with my ex-husband and his divine new fiancée," I said. As soon as I said it, I regretted it. I planned *not* to mention this, because I thought it might upset Claire, especially since Burke's fiancée was packing it up in L.A. and moving to Washington for him, and this was well known.

It did upset her.

"What will I do when that moment comes, when I have to meet Jess and his new fiancée?" Claire said. "Oh God, I'm hyperventilating."

"Take your head off," Tamayo said. "Breathe deep. Sometimes people are only meant to take each other partway in life."

"Where'd you hear that?" I asked.

"From your super," Tamayo said. "Phil. I had tea with him and Helen after my tarot reading. Claire, you should call Sally. Have a tarot with her, and then have tea with Phil. Pick you right up."

"Don't call Sally," I said, exasperated.

Sally would give Claire the usual rap about following her instincts. We all have good and bad instincts, so you can't follow all of them, though Sally certainly tried. Her instincts led her to Dirk, a writer in his second year of writer's block who kicked her naked out of his apartment one night and refused to let her back in to get her clothes and books, despite Sally's screaming and banging on his door.

When she finally got her stuff back, it had all been mutilated by Dirk. Big chunks were cut out of clothes, the CDs were cracked and scratched, and pages were missing from her books. Sally spent a month trying to piece together what was on those missing pages, thinking it was some coded message from Dirk and if she figured it out

she won some kind of big prize, like the return of his af-
fection. She didn't give up this quest until she met a new
True Love, the one who took off with her life savings.

"You know how Sally makes decisions," I said. "When
the tarot and the horoscope don't provide the answer, she
tells herself: If I see a red car before a blue car, I'll do *A*.
If I see a blue car before a red car, I'll do *B*. It's hardly a
rational process you can invest faith in."

"You don't get it," Tamayo said.

We got a cab, and as we rode uptown Claire snapped
herself out of her angst by resuming her questioning about
Julie. How come Julie had waited so long to contact me?

"We had a falling-out, a long time ago. You know how
it is when you're young. You harbor grudges over dumb
stuff. Then you grow up and get nostalgic and you let go
of the shit and reconnect. You'll know what I mean in
about ten years."

Claire rolled her eyes. She hates it when I play the age
and experience cards, but I had about a decade of experience on her, things I'd learned the hard way, like, a little
religion can come in handy sometimes, a cat is a woman's
best friend, and if you attend an airborne ash-scattering
keep your mouth shut and beware the updraft, among
other things.

"What did you fall out over?"

"A dress I borrowed and returned in less-than-ideal
shape."

"Pretty dumb thing to nurse a grudge over."

"Hey, people are killed for less," Tamayo said. "Right,
Robin? Tell her about the chicken and the egg."

Buried somewhere in my closet is a box of scrapbooks
full of stories about people who killed each other for less,
entitled "The Straw That Broke the Camel's Back," e.g., the
man who killed his wife in an argument over where to put

the mustard on the dinner table. People have been killed ostensibly because they served eggs for breakfast every single day, because they hid the milk behind the vegetables in the refrigerator, in arguments over toast and marmalade, etc. In the Philippines, two brothers fought to the death in an argument over who was prettier, Imelda Marcos or Princess Diana. The Imelda man won.

"Remember the woman who killed her husband with a skillet because he 'forgot' to mow the lawn for the third day in a row?" Tamayo said.

"I'm sure there was more to it than the lawn," Claire said, and she was right. The woman who hit her husband in the head fifty-some times with a skillet, hammering him like a nail, didn't do it because of the lawn. She did it because she suddenly decided she'd like him a whole lot better a foot shorter and dead. That Filipino brother didn't die over the debatable charms of Princess Diana. Same with the woman killed over mustard placement on the dinner table. The real issues weren't condiments or Imelda Marcos, because what goddamned difference does it make? Those are the cover arguments for the real issues.

"Isn't it funny how people would rather kill each other than be honest and work things out?" I said.

"It's fucking hilarious," Claire said. "But there's got to be more to it than just a stained dress. I hope we're not wasting an evening because of her."

"Yeah, there better be a payoff," Tamayo said. "There better be major fun waiting for us."

My first inclination was to keep mum, maybe pout a bit, think to myself that it would be good to see a real friend, like Julie, who understood me.

But I had to admit there was resentment between us.

"There was probably a lot of stuff going on that I didn't understand at the time," I said. "I think some of it had to do with Doug Gribetz, this boy we were both in love with when we were growing up. Between me and Julie, it became untenable, our both having a crush on the same boy, so we solved the problem by betting on him in a game of Trouble. That was Julie's idea."

"Oh, my older sister had that game. With the Pop-o-Matic, right?" Claire said.

"Pop-o-what?" Tamayo said.

"Dice in a plastic bubble. You popped the bubble to roll the dice," I explained.

"That's the kind of thing I wanted!" Tamayo said. "I love my Grandma Scheinman, but she never got the girl stuff right. I'd ask for American toys for Hanukkah or my birthday and she'd send me porcelain dolls and Parcheesi games."

"Poor Tamayo," Claire said. She turned to me. "You bet this boy in a game of Trouble?"

"Yeah, the winner got to be in love with Doug Gribetz, the loser got to be in love with Bobby Sherman. And we adored Bobby Sherman, especially Julie. . . ."

"Bobby Sherman?" Tamayo said.

"He sang the song, 'Julie Do You Love Me,' " Claire said.

"Julie loved that Julie song. That should give you some idea how wonderful Doug Gribetz was, that the winner got to be in love with him over Bobby Sherman. Anyway, I lost. I know that sounds hilarious, but it was a big issue between us for years. At least for me."

Doug Gribetz. Even now that name made my heart beat faster. He was the standard by which I judged all other men, and all other men fell short. It was completely understandable that I was in love with him. Every girl was in love with Doug Gribetz. Hard not to be. It wasn't just that he was nice-looking and smart. In a lot of ways, he was the most mature boy I'd ever known. Popular with everyone because he was kind to everyone, even me, and everyone respected him. He had a good heart. We rarely spoke in all the years we shared a classroom, but one time, in third grade, when I was being pushed roughly around a circle of girls, he came up and said, "What are you doing?" in a voice that made all the girls stop and hang their heads a little. He walked me home, and we talked about stuff the whole way. I was on cloud nine. We parted shyly, and never spoke extensively again. After that, I was never tortured by the popular girls while he was present. Did that ever deepen my infatuation.

"Julie ended up dating Doug for a while in eleventh grade. That really burned my butt," I said.

"What other resentments did you have?" Claire asked.

"Oh gee. Let me think. I resented that she was prettier than me, or at least always acted like she was, and she resented that I got better grades in school even though she thought she was smarter than me, especially in math and stuff like that. That was all a long time ago. It seems so silly now. What we shared was so much greater than the things that tore us apart," I said.

There was more to our resentment than I was willing to admit to Claire and Tamayo.

"I think she's trying to show you how rich she is and how smart she is, that she can get you going this way," Tamayo said as we pulled up to a nondescript building with an awning on Park Avenue.

Way to go, Julie, I thought. You managed to get that Park Avenue address, one way or another.

☼ 13 ☼

PARK AVENUE is a grand boulevard with a tree-lined concrete divider that stretches from Union Square downtown up into East Harlem. From Grand Central to the 90s, it is an aberrant stretch of quiet in New York, super-ritzy, with clean, broad sidewalks, buildings with doormen, bright lights, very few shops, and a rather snotty attitude designed to keep the city's less hygienic riffraff at bay. Even at this late hour, you could almost choke on the smell of White Shoulders perfume and old money in the air.

The doorman didn't know who we were and there was no answer on the house phone, which supported my theory that the party was elsewhere, that Kathy had come here after she'd run into Julie and been drawn into the prank and they'd gone on from here. We made up a big story, about our friend Kathy, a cleaning woman who we feared had fallen into a diabetic coma and was stuck in a closet. But the doorman either didn't believe us or wasn't anxious to let a trio of strange women in costume up into his building, and he couldn't leave his post to accompany us.

"Parking garage," Claire said. We went around the corner to the building's garage entrance, and waited about five minutes before the garage door rolled open and one of the tenants drove out. As casually as possible, we walked in under the closing door. From there, we caught the elevator.

The apartment was on the eleventh floor. There was no answer to our knocks, but the door was slightly open, exposing about a quarter-inch of the door jamb. It gave easily with a firm push.

For a moment, I forgot this was all a big joke, and felt alarmed. Then, I remembered, and laughed. Claire and Tamayo, who had been waiting for my emotional cue, laughed too.

Claire said, "I think they're waiting for us."

The door opened into a beautiful apartment, as cold as a meat locker. The A/C was cranked up full and there was the scent of aftershave in the air, something expensive with a woodsy cedar undernote, like Chanel Antaeus. The place was decorated with country antiques, the very expensive kind, lots of rough-hewn blond wood cabinets and things with appliqué. Expensive, and yet comfortable.

"Hello?" I called out. There was no answer.

Claire called. Nothing.

"There's nobody here," Tamayo said, going into the kitchen. Claire and I went into the bedroom, which was similarly furnished, right down to the antique blue ceramic pitcher and basin on the bedside table. You would have thought you were in nineteenth-century Provence if it weren't for the desk with the computer on it. Didn't seem like Julie's taste, though, at least not the *old* Julie, the one I knew. If she had money, and evidently she did, I figured she'd go way overboard, lots of rococo gilt and crystal chandeliers, like a smaller version of the Plaza Hotel after it was Ivana-ized.

This sure was a long way from the basement suite in the house where Julie and her mom lived with Julie's uncle and his common-law wife. From a grim gray carpet, stained in spots and musty-smelling from the floods every spring, to this, a blue-and-gold Qum carpet worth tens of thousands of dollars. From cast-off square brown furniture with frayed edges to French country antiques, and instead of the cheap print showing covered bridges and mountain vistas, numbered prints by trendy artists.

"Maybe it doesn't belong to Julie. Maybe it belongs to this Anne Winston person," Claire said.

In the closet, there was nothing but a giant clown costume hanging on a wooden hanger and two big red floppy shoes. On the floor just outside the closet was a telephone, which had big number buttons, all lit up. We followed the cord to the answering machine on the desk.

"Check it," Claire said. I pushed the replay button.

The first message was from Kathy: "Hi, I work for Robin Hudson and I've been following clues in the murder mystery you set up. I am outside a place called Joy II and I think there has been a mistake. . . ."

"Hello?" said a man's voice on the machine. Then the machine clicked off.

After that were two messages from me.

"A man answered, not your friend Julie," Claire said.

"One of Julie's charitable co-conspirators, I guess," I said.

"Should we snoop?" Tamayo asked, poised at a desk drawer.

"We shouldn't," I said. "But . . ."

Before I could finish my sentence, Tamayo and Claire were opening drawers and looking for things. A lot of the drawers were completely empty. There were magazines: *Town & Country, Architectural Digest, People, Vogue, Forbes, Business Week*, and a few obscure financial journals. We found bill stubs, all to Help for Kids, some underwear and snagged pantyhose, a few unmatched socks, and some sundry items. Though plugged in, the computer didn't turn on. It had either been locked or was out of order.

We went into the bathroom, which reeked of aftershave. On the floor near the toilet was a rubber clown mask, the kind that covers the whole head. Clowns are creepy and give me the chills anyway, but a disembodied clown face can really send a rat running up your trouser leg.

There was one toothbrush, pretty worn down, the bristles yellowed. Inside the medicine cabinet was a half-box of Tampax and a half-bottle of expired aspirin, in the wastebasket a used Mennen Speed Stick and shards of a broken aftershave bottle. I'd nailed it: Chanel Antaeus. Normally, I prefer a man's natural smell, but I do love Antaeus.

"It's like someone moved out and left their furniture behind," Claire said. "Maybe they're changing offices."

"And apartments. People live here too," Tamayo said.

"Yeah, looks like Julie . . . or someone . . . has been living here with a man," I said.

"Beautiful bathroom," Claire said, pulling the shower curtain around the old-fashioned footed bathtub.

"Fuckeroo!" she gasped.

There was a body in the tub, a man, his knees brought up to his chest. We only got a quick gander, and then we heard someone coming in.

"Hide," Claire said.

In a bad imitation of a Three Stooges routine, we all three tried to cram through the bathroom door at once on our way to the bedroom. We scrambled under the bed. The bedspread hung down almost to the floor, and we could see only about a quarter-inch beneath it.

The bathroom door closed and a man said something nonsensical that sounded like, "Here's the hamburger." There was some muffled thumping, but I couldn't tell if that was the men or my heart, and then we heard the sound of water running. A creak. The bathroom door opened. The slamming of metal on metal. More thumping. The front door closed. Silence.

After a few minutes of tense waiting to make sure the coast was clear, we poked our heads out from under the bed, and looked at each other.

"Fuck," Claire said, and she went back into the bathroom.

The body was gone.

"Call the cops," Tamayo said.

"We can't call the cops from here," Claire said.

Claire and Tamayo were wide-eyed and freaking out. I just stood back and let them go at it.

"Why?" Tamayo asked.

"Aside from the fact that we have no body, we can't identify the men who came in, and we're guilty of a B&E," Claire said, "what about our reputations? And somehow Kathy and Robin's friend Julie are mixed up in this, so we have to think about this before we do anything that might put them in danger. I don't know what to do. Shit. This could destroy me as a journalist."

"Claire, it isn't what . . ." I tried to say, but she didn't even acknowledge me. I'd never seen her in such a panicky state, leaping to conclusions, so unsure what to do.

"We didn't B, we only E'd," Tamayo said. "We came in here very innocently, expecting Julie and Kathy."

"Let's get the hell out of here," Claire said. "I can't think in here. Fuck. Fuck. Fuck."

She took off out of the apartment and down the stairwell, not waiting for us, like she was following some weird voice in her head. Tamayo and I looked at each other, and then followed. We left the way we came.

"Thank God, you're both wearing gloves, and I have paws," Claire said. "No prints. So, even if someone saw us through their peepholes or when we were going into the garage, the best they can give the cops is a physical description."

"Imagine that APB," Tamayo said. "Be on the lookout for a giant dog, a vampire with a red 'fro, and Marilyn Monroe."

"There's no reason to panic. This probably isn't what it looks like, trust me," I said, pushing the garage exit button. As we walked quickly away from the building towards Lexington Avenue, I said, "You're operating on the assumption he was dead or likely dead. This is part of the joke. I've already had a dead harlequin come back to life on me tonight. It's another Goomey-style red herring. It's too convincing."

"Too convincing?"

"It is if you think like Julie Goomey. So far, she's used a real charity, real merchants, sent actors and possibly a male escort to deliver messages. . . ."

"Robin, I don't think that was a joke," Claire said.

"He was so pale, he looked pretty dead to me. But, then, so does Robin," Tamayo said.

"Claire, I think that was George the rich guy. I recognized him by his distinctive flaring nostrils."

"That was George the rich guy?" Tamayo said.

"He looked familiar to me too, Robin," Claire said. "I'm sure I read a story about him this week. Damn, I sure wish I'd paid more attention to the stories I was reading."

"You don't pay attention?"

"The funny thing about marathon anchoring, Rob, is that after the third hour you don't even hear the stories you're reading. Didn't you watch the news this week?"

"I didn't have time in L.A. I was too busy going to screenings and visiting old friends." And old husbands, I added silently.

I pulled one of the photos out of my bag, the one I'd picked up at Backslash, showing George with Julie. "See?

Here he is. This was taken when we came to New York. He's older now, but looks a lot the same."

"That does look like him," Claire said. She studied the picture closely. "It says September 1979 on the side of this photo. See here? The printed date?"

"Yeah."

"Didn't you say you came to New York for spring break?"

"Yeah. So she didn't get it developed until later. Or she had prints made in the fall. But you see, it's part of the joke, the trip down memory lane. . . ."

"You're sure it's just Julie's sick joke."

"Yeah. Trust me."

"He was such a weird white color . . ." Tamayo said. "But there was no smell, except for that aftershave smell, so he couldn't have been dead long. Maybe he was just passed out."

"With his eyes open?" Claire said. "The apartment was cold, so the body would stay cold and decompose more slowly."

"Maybe he was wearing Halloween makeup. We didn't get a good look at him," I said. "He heard us come in. Played dead in the tub. Then his friends came in and they left."

"Why would he have makeup on if he was going to wear the clown mask? Unless someone else was wearing the clown mask . . . God, breaking and entering, failing to report a possible crime . . . if I'd known . . . God, I'm a felon. An unconvicted felon," Claire said.

"What are we going to do now?" Tamayo asked.

"There's a pay phone," Claire said. "We'll call the cops, anonymously, report a possible murder. Maybe they'll find some evidence in the apartment or something."

"That's exactly what Julie would like you to do," I said,

but stood back quietly as Claire made a hysterical anonymous phone call.

"Before we go any further, Robin, I need to know what you did to Julie that would make her fuck with you so much and make you jump to her tune all night," Claire said. "It's got to be a lot more than a stained dress and a game of Trouble."

Though I hated to admit it to Tamayo and Claire, I had fucked Julie over, a long time ago. Would Julie nurse a grudge for almost twenty years? I knew in the past she'd nursed a grudge or two—so had I. But we were the same age, so she must have gone through the same midlife crap I'd gone through in the past few years, questioning one's choices, letting go of a lot of the crap, coming to terms with one's limitations, forgiving, within reason, and forgetting.

But that forgetting part, it can get you into trouble.

I took a deep breath, started to say something, stopped, and took another deep breath, before I finally said, "I told you how Julie and I were in love with the same boy for years, Doug Gribetz, but I lost Doug Rights in a game of Trouble? Okay. Well, Julie finally went out with Doug Gribetz in eleventh grade. I was jealous, I guess. So, I did this thing to her."

"What?"

"I kind of caused her breakup with Doug. I ratted Julie out to Doug—not directly, but through his friend Lance, who had a crush on Julie—after she cheated on Doug in Minneapolis. Lance let something slip, and I knew he would, because he always had a thing for Julie and had chased her for years. She didn't find out that I was the one who ratted her out until a few years later, after we came back from New York. It's terrible, I know. I'm sorry you have to see that side of me. But it was a long time ago."

"We forgive you," Claire said, dryly.

"What do we do now?" Tamayo said.

"I'm not sure. The last clue I got was 'neon hand,' which alludes to a woman we saw. . . ."

"Why didn't you tell me that before? It's a bar-restaurant, vegetarian, New Age, in your neighborhood," Tamayo said.

"Really?" I hadn't been out much around the neighborhood lately and I couldn't keep up with all the new places, not since the hit Broadway show *Rent* had made the neighborhood extra-trendy.

"It's on St. Mark's," she said. "Pretty new. About two months old. It was really hip about a month ago but it's on the downside of the trend now."

"You go to Neon Hand, Rob. I'm going back to ANN, look through the fax photos, find out who this guy George is, run a couple more checks on Julie Goomey," Claire said. "Tamayo, why don't you come with me. I'll get you a cell phone from the assignment desk. You can check out Julie Goomey's old apartment building, see what her old neighbors have to say about her. Then we can rendezvous."

Claire was getting a grip. So miserable just an hour before, she was now energized by my problem, and reclaiming her authority, which boosted my confidence considerably.

"Synchronize your watches," she said.

We thought she was kidding.

"Synchronize your watches. After all the missed connections tonight, we don't want to take any chances."

We synchronized our watches.

❖ 14 ❖

As I RODE the Lexington Avenue local down to Astor Place, I thought about what Claire had said about Julie fucking with me. Claire was so suspicious that she now had me really wondering about Julie. I went back and forth for a while, with all the voices in my head arguing different sides of the question.

But, no, I decided, not after all we went through together, fatherlessness, daffy mothers, cooties, and redeeming those cooties to become semipopular.

Even though I look back on my shallow, semipopular high-school years with significant regret and embarrassment, I am still kind of proud that we were able to transform ourselves in one summer, and still grateful to Julie, because she was the engine behind it. Before she moved to Ferrous, she had been popular, or so she claimed, and it became her life's work to get back her previous lofty social status. I had never been popular—I had always been considered weird—and, not knowing any different, I didn't know just how bad a thing that was until Julie arrived. It was her deep shame at her cooties that made me aware of my own shame.

Several things helped us redeem our cooties. Our junior high school fed into a huge high school serving five towns, four of which had no knowledge of our previous cootie status. That gave us a nearly fresh sheet of paper with which to start high school, reputation-wise. It also helped that our enemies, Mary and Sis, were going away to some horsey private boarding school in Virginia.

So, the summer before high school, we dieted, using a

candy called Ayds that we ordered from the back of a trashy magazine. We exercised like crazy and practiced gymnastics and dance so we could go out for junior cheer-leaders. We started wearing makeup, Julie got contact lenses, and I started relaxing my hair to give me a more sultry Rita Hayworth look, the Farrah style being beyond what I could accomplish. We read Susan Dey's book about how to be popular. In preparation for dating, we even prac-ticed closed-mouth necking with Julie's cousin Jack when he came to visit. There was no French kissing—which is fortunate, because it would have been creepy to French-kiss Julie's cousin, who was a full year younger and a twerp. (The practice kissing came to a halt when the little prick tried to cop a feel.)

So many different images of Julie went through my head. Some of them made me crack up, like Julie dressed in her pirate costume. She loved to play pirates, and so did I. People still have this goofy idea about girlhood, even other women, which I find inexplicable, that girls of my gener-ation spent all their time in frilly dresses drinking tea from tiny cups across the table from their dolls, or wheeling dolls in doll carriages and combing the hair on their Barbie dolls with tiny Barbie-doll combs. Dolls were such a small part of most girls' experience. Most of the time, we were riding our bikes, playing cops and robbers, pirates, softball, climb-ing trees, doing homework, or torturing each other, just like boys.

Then, for Julie and me, there was the whole bandit-queen thing. I had to laugh when I thought about Julie dressed up like Putli Bai, in polyester tunic and harem pants, full makeup, jewelry, with a toy gun in her hand and a fierce expression on her face. Somewhere, I had a picture of that. On the back of it, she had scrawled, "Be all that you can be."

That was her favorite role to play, bandit queen. Leading an army of men and sometimes women. Beholden to nobody but the gods and goddesses. Stealing from the rich, giving to the poor. What really got Julie was that Putli Bai was shot dead in January 1958, a few days before Julie was born. Julie thought that was somehow significant.

As I came out of the subway station at Astor Place, a film crew was there shooting a movie, a period piece set in the 1960s, judging by the costumes and the cars. It looked almost like the real Astor, just off enough to make me uneasy. There were actors, spectators, and lots of film people with walkie-talkies and clipboards. I walked through the faux Astor, passing through fantasy on my way back to reality. That seemed an apt metaphor for the blurring of reality and fantasy tonight. When I entered the faux Astor, I was still trying to give Julie the benefit of the doubt, convincing myself that her intentions were good, if misguided.

By the time I got to the other side of the faux Astor, my view had changed. In between, I heard one of the guys with walkie-talkies say, "Ginger, can you bring some scrim?"

One time, late at night, when most good kids and good parents were in bed, we were playing a game known variously as Ring and Run and Knock a Door Ginger at Mrs. Johannsen's house. We were thirteen.

Though I was usually up for Julie's pranks, this one gave me pause, because Mrs. Johannsen's husband was away on business in Duluth, and Mrs. J. was home alone. I didn't want to scare her. But Julie said, "Don't worry."

We rang the doorbell several times, and then hid behind the caragana hedge. The curtain opened in the little diamond window on the front door. Then nothing.

Julie ran back up to the house and rang the doorbell

again a bunch of times. At the time, I remember thinking, She's crazy. She's gonna get caught. I almost hightailed it out of there then. I would have, if I hadn't been frozen in place.

This time, instead of coming back, Julie hid by the side of the house, peeking at the back door. I stuck my head up, trying to signal Julie, and when I did, Mrs. J.'s face was in the diamond window, staring at me. I'd been caught. I started walking towards the back alley, as casually as possible, whistling out the side of my mouth for Julie, trying to signal her to meet me in the alley. I looked back. The curtain was closed.

I was stationed in the alley, Julie behind the house. She saw me and put her finger to her mouth. The back porch door opened and a man came out. It was Mr. Groddeck, who owned the Ford dealership on the interstate.

When Julie saw him, she said, "Hello, Mr. Groddeck," and then she took off like a bat out of hell to the alley, grabbing my hand and saying, "Come on."

Groddeck chased us for two blocks, but somehow we got away. I was scared shitless Groddeck would call the school, or my mother, or, worse, my Aunt Maureen. But he didn't. In fact, every time he saw Julie or me after that, he smiled and gave us money.

"He's really a nice guy," was Julie's explanation.

So nice that one night in high school, when Julie was feeling her oats, as they say, and she stole a car from the Groddeck Motors lot, Mr. Groddeck didn't press charges. It's terrible, but I had to laugh at Julie's nerve. Her uncle, with whom she lived, was an auto mechanic, and Julie picked up a lot from him, including how to hot-wire a car. One night, she showed up outside my house, honking her horn. She'd "borrowed" a car and wanted to take me for a drive, cruise the boys in Newton. We hit every hangout in Five Towns before the cops grabbed us on the interstate, frisked us and everything. Julie told the cops she'd just borrowed the car, that Mr. Groddeck knew about it, and when the cops told Groddeck who was involved, he apologized, said of course he'd told Julie she could borrow a car, and we were released. Only afterwards did Julie gleefully confess that she had stolen the car, and she knew Groddeck was "too much of a sap" to charge her. I was kind of ticked about her putting me through that, but there was something exhilarating and outlaw about it too.

Now I was completely pissed off. Now I understood. Julie knew that Groddeck would be at Mrs. Johannsen's house that night. She and I were blackmailing him and didn't even know it. Or I didn't, at least. Julie obviously did. She'd enjoyed making Groddeck twist in the wind like that. Maybe it had something to do with her dad. Maybe she was just cruel. But she milked Groddeck for a long time, and he gave her a job doing his books after she graduated from high school.

Who was she now?

Suddenly, I had to question everything. What else had I misunderstood, misinterpreted? That note she brought to sewing class in eighth grade, ostensibly from the principal —it seemed so hilarious at the time. But what if Old Hobnail had insisted on reading it? I could have been in a lot of trouble because of that. Still, it was funny. Telling George and Billy I spoke French, setting me up like that, that wasn't too nice. Yet that too was pretty funny.

But that note she typed and signed "Doug Gribetz," that was downright cruel. Getting my hopes up for a brief moment, then telling me she wrote it. Man, that was mean. There was nothing funny about that.

This was a pretty mean joke too. I'm pretty good at seeing the hidden menace in things. But I'm not always so good at seeing the hidden menace in people.

How could I hold it against her, though? She'd had such a shitty childhood. Julie's mother would bring strange men home, men she met at her brother's gas station on the interstate. The men would give Julie money to go away, and she'd show up at my place at all hours with money in her pocket. Get-lost money, she called it. She'd climb up the fire ladder to my window and knock. More than once, we'd gone out after my curfew to ring doorbells or smoke cigarettes with dark-eyed juvenile-delinquent boys behind the elementary school.

And here I was again, thirty-eight years old and out after curfew because of Julie. Despite the late hour, or maybe because of it, St. Mark's Place—which is, numerically, East 8th Street—was fully alive. The colored carnival lights strung up and down the street for Halloween created a corridor of artificial brightness through the darkness. This street never sleeps, at least not at night. The lights were still stark in the T-shirt and earring shops, in Cappuccino & Tattoo and the leather bondage-clothes place, dim inside the bars and coffeehouses. The sidewalks were full of people, a lot of them in costume waiting to get into late-night joints. Punked-out kids were clustered outside Coney Island High, a retro punk-rock club. Homeless guys sold books and magazines and other stuff from card tables. Tamayo once said this neighborhood's nocturnal commerce made her think of the last carnival on a dying star, a feeling intensified tonight by all the people in bizarre costumes.

"Beware the asparagus," some nutball screamed as he ran past me.

Loony toons? Or ahead of the curve?

About thirty years ago, I remember seeing some nutball

standing on a corner in Duluth raving about how spray cans were going to burn a hole in the sky, and people thought he was toons. We put everything in spray cans, shaving cream, hairspray, even cheese. Then we found out how fluorocarbons in spray products helped destroy the ozone. So that guy wasn't crazy, at least not about the spray cans. He was just ahead of the curve. After you've lived long enough, you gotta wonder which things that serve and delight us today will turn around on us later. When I was a kid, figure skaters were national sweethearts, postal workers were noble, sleet-fighting heroes, spray cans were the greatest invention since sliced bread, and Julie Goomey was my bosom buddy.

15

Neon Hand was attached to a pagan-witchcraft store. There was a big neon hand in its window, just like the kind in gypsy fortune-teller windows, only at the Neon Hand it was flanked by a neon Budweiser bottle on one side and the word "Guinness" in red on the other.

I went to the bar to see if the bartender knew what was going on, and she didn't, though she signed me up to speak with the resident fortune-teller, who was "scrying" with someone in a back room at the moment and wouldn't be available for a while. Scrying, I knew from Sally, is the ancient art of staring into crystals or other shiny surfaces in order to receive prophetic visions. It was perfected by Nostradamus.

It was a lighthearted kind of place, Neon Hand, no pentagrams, or anything too dark and creepy, in this joint. The place was decorated in very soothing pale green. Aside from the bar lights, the only lights were hundreds of rows of tiny Christmas bulbs in soft pastel colors, pink, yellow, blue, green, and white, blending to give the room an iridescent cast. There were shelves filled with books about magic, and old-fashioned looking jars of herbs, and the walls were lined with an eclectic selection of magic celebrity photos. Most of them I recognized—Aleister Crowley, Gerald B. Gardner, Austin O. Spare, even Elizabeth Montgomery, Sabrina, and Kim Novak. It was a Gen-X/Y bar, so you had to expect a few ironic pop-cultural references to lighten things up.

"I know you," said a man leaning on the bar. "Small world. You look different, though. . . ."

It was Greg, a guy we'd interviewed for our ANN special report on the paranormal. He heads a group of middle-aged warlocks called the Viziers, who use their "magical powers" to get twenty-year-old women to sleep with them, which my neighbor Sally saw as a shameful squandering of power and I saw as just plain nuts.

"Yeah. Robin Hudson, ANN. I'm sorry. I don't have time to talk right now. . . ."

"Aw, you have time to talk to me." The guy fancied himself to have quite a mesmerizing stare, and he fixed his eyes on me, like he was trying to make me fall under his spell. As if staring into his eyes would somehow block my brain, my libido, my peripheral vision, and, most important, my sense of smell, since he had breath like the inside of Jeffrey Dahmer's refrigerator.

I was a *tad* over the hill for this loser, and I looked like a redheaded version of an unholy mating between Don King and Madeline Kahn (at the end of *Young Franken-stein*), but it was late, he was drunk and obviously desperate. Funny thing, though: When I'd met him out of costume during our special report, when I was a lot more attractive, he hadn't vibed to me at all. Now I looked dead and he was all charged up. Maybe he had a thing for dead girls.

What a lousy time to get hit on. Because I suspected that magic had less to do with whatever conquests this guy could claim than Pfizer, I was careful to watch my seltzer and lime as the bartender brought it to me. What I didn't need right now—any time, but especially right now—was Dr. Bombay slipping a roofie or 'lude or something into my seltzer. Roofies, or date-rape pills, are many times stronger than Valium and have the scary side effect of inducing temporary amnesia, so you don't even remember what happened. I didn't need one. I felt like I'd been under the influence of one for twenty-plus years.

"I can't talk right now," I said, more insistently. "I'm waiting for someone."

"Waiting for me?"

"No, I'm not waiting for you."

I stopped.

Maybe I *was* waiting for him.

"Do you know Julie Goomey?" I asked. "Or Anne Winston?"

"Should I?" he said.

"Do you have a clue for me?"

"I have a clue for you right here," he said, putting his hand on his crotch.

Loser. No wonder he needed "magic" to meet women.

"A woman doesn't generally go into a bar alone unless she's looking for something," he said.

"Yeah, a seltzer and a seat alone," I said, walking away to a booth, thinking, Right, gotta go, the microchip in my buttocks is beeping. Amazing. It's the nineties, and a woman still can't walk into a pub to quaff a refreshment without its being seen by some dinosaur as a blatant attempt to get laid. Every time I thought the human race was evolving, I'd meet some Missing Link who'd been left behind—and who was probably spreading his seed around and polluting the gene pool.

I wanted to say to the guy, Why don't you just lose the magic and whatever else you use and just talk to women? Why do you have to control them? Don't you want to find a nice woman your own age who shares your interests and appreciates you for who you are?

But then I remembered that I am the last person who should be giving advice.

The place smelled faintly of burning herbs. Not too

much, though. It's a floral, funereal smell that wears on you quickly, I've found, and the Neon Hand had dealt with this by burning all spells in closed fireplaces that vented upward through charcoal filters, installed because of neighbor complaints.

According to the booklet about magic tucked into the menu at my table, there was always a fortune-teller on duty at Neon Hand to do palms, tea leaves, computer astrological charts, even mix a "nontoxic"—i.e., positive—spell for you. Black magic was not allowed.

I was hungry again, so I ordered a veggie burger. More out of nervousness than anything else, I read through the booklet, a brochure really, while I ate. The cover bore a drawing of a woman identified as Hecate, goddess of the dark side of the moon, queen of ghosts and other dark and hidden things, ruler of magic and wisdom. Did that ever resonate with me tonight.

"Magic," the booklet said, "is understanding of, cooperation with, and respect for nature. Traditional Science is the attempted manipulation and mastery of nature." Scientists were at this very moment growing human hair in test tubes and human ears on the backs of white mice without immune systems, concocting all sorts of molecular monstrosities meant to approximate fat, and combining genes from pigs and tomatoes. I couldn't help thinking how provident this last could be. Add a lettuce gene and you have a BLT. Or combine a gene from those French pigs that sniff out truffles with a gene from the truffle, and create a truffle that finds itself.

Lucky truffle.

Meanwhile, the booklet went on ominously, auspicious albino crocodiles appear in Cambodia, a thousand-mile column of migrating toads makes its way through provincial China, a green cat is born in Denmark, bunches of frogs shower down from the sky in several places in Scotland, and in Iowa a farmer reports a cow who tracks, captures, and eats chickens. Here in New York, coyotes roam the Bronx, wild boars had been sighted in Staten Island and Queens, and a large alligator was pulled from a pond in Brooklyn. Mother Nature is coming back, the booklet warned.

And, boy, is she pissed.

Just then someone said, "Hi, Robin, how are you?"

It was Sally, standing by my booth.

"Hi, Sally. I'm fine. You?"

"Well, the PMS medication I've been taking has caused a slight numbness in my left arm. . . ."

"So I've heard."

"And I broke up with Joshua. Actually, he broke up with me."

"Who is Joshua?"

"Oh, you didn't meet him. He was my most recent boyfriend. Robin, why can't I meet a nice guy?"

I wanted to tell her—Sally, get into therapy and grow your hair out to cover your baldness and your tattoo. You have a big scorpion up the back of your bald head! Some men, believe it or not, consider this a turnoff. But I didn't know how to tell her this without hurting her feelings and sending her off the deep end, and subtler expressions of this sentiment missed their mark. For a week in the spring, she'd worn a wig, and she looked very pretty with hair, which I mentioned to her. But that phase didn't last long.

The one time I was able to get her to talk about her appearance, she told me that the man of her dreams would see through to her soul and that's how she'd know he was the right one, which sounds lovely in theory, except a succession of right ones had come through her doorway and turned out to be wrong. Despite all my subtle and non-subtle hints, she refused to see a shrink, though she did consult with one of her nutty gurus, Sister Delia, a reader of past lives whose real name was Norma Finsecker.

"I dunno, Sal. I'm the wrong person to ask. What are you doing here?"

"I'm waiting for someone. And while I was waiting I was assisting the resident fortune-teller. It's been busy tonight—Halloween and all. Hey, you know what? I saw Louise Bryant about an hour ago. At the window here."

"Oh," I said. "No shit."

"What are you doing here?"

"I'm waiting for someone too."

"Who are you waiting for?"

"I don't know." I suddenly got it. "Who are you waiting for?"

"Somebody to pick up an envelope for a murder mystery," she said.

"Who hired you to do this?"

"I can't tell you."

"Sally, this is a scam, and my intern Kathy has been sucked up into it, so you'd better tell me what you know."

Sally chewed her lower lip. "Her name is Anne Winston. She's a client and had become a friend. Don't you remember? I mentioned her last week, the friend I wanted to bring along tonight. But she said she couldn't make it, and then she hired me to do this delivery."

"I remember you mentioning a friend, the one who was having an affair with a guy who was going to jail, and the wife was on to them. But I don't remember you mentioning her name," I said, as I opened the envelope.

"Psychic-client privilege," she said. Ever since I chewed her out for telling people she advised me, she had been keeping client names confidential. It was her theory now that you could tell anything about someone as long as you didn't reveal who the person was.

"You've met her, this Anne?"

"Yes. She came by a few times. Mostly we talked on the phone, for two months, maybe a little more. She read about me in the newspaper."

"She read about *me*," I said. I was catching on. "She read that I was one of your ostensible clients. She was coming to you to get info about me."

The envelope contained a key, a newspaper clipping, and a cryptic clue. The story, from summer 1991, was about the bones of a Perrugia-family thug, Frankie "the Fish" DeMarco, being found in the old Brooklyn dunes. The guy had been a numbers runner, a hijacker, a procurer, and was suspected of a couple of hits before he vanished. He'd been missing for over a decade. It jarred me. Was there really a murder? Or was this another red herring?

"Who the hell is Frankie the Fish?" I asked. Sally didn't know.

The clue was baffling. "Grand Four-Eyes cousin with leg braces." At first I didn't get what Julie was trying to say with this gratuitously strange imagery. I wracked my brain trying to come up with associations or allusions that decoded it, but it made no sense. It sounded like something that was badly translated from English into a completely incompatible language like Hindi, and then translated (badly) back into English.

"Do you know what this key fits?" I asked Sally.

"No."

"What did she look like? Anne Winston."

"Pretty, a blonde . . ."

"Dye job? Wig?"

"I don't know. Maybe."

"Did she pay by credit card?"

"Cash."

"Did she talk about me?"

"Not by name. I never identified you by name."

Well, that was big of her. It would be so hard to figure out who Sally's unnamed redheaded friend who worked in twenty-four-hour news was.

"Whatever. She knew we were all going to go out tonight. She knew it was a Girls' Night Out."

"Yeah," she said.

"And this envelope came to you by FedEx today?"

"How did you know?"

I'm a fucking psychic, I thought, but didn't say. I filled Sally in on what had gone down, watching her expression grow sadder and more alarmed. When Sally's face grew sad, it was heartbreaking. I thought to myself, I bet she had super-cooties when she was a kid.

"Anne Winston is Julie Goomey," I said. Julie might have had a co-conspirator named Anne who worked with her at this perverse charity, but Julie wouldn't send someone else to get info on me from Sally. She'd have too much fun doing it herself.

"I was so sure about her. I was so sure about what I saw for her. How could I be so wrong?"

"You're only human."

"I fucked it up. I am so worthless. . . . I am such a fraud."

"Sally, everyone makes mistakes."

"Now I know what my orange dream means. It means I'm a fraud."

"The orange dream?"

"I dreamed I invented the orange. I didn't have any money for the subway, so I gave the token clerk my orange, and he threw it onto the tracks. A big rat came and took

it and it was gone. And it was the only orange in existence."
At this, she burst into tears.

Suddenly, I realized that, in some weird way, Sally was
right to shave her head and have a scorpion up the back
of it. It was right for her to express herself. She was weird
and tough (scorpion), vulnerable and exposed (bald head).
Now that I thought about it, this suited her. When Sally
was completely insane in the spring, after her cat, Pie, died
and her then True Love pulled a gun on her and took off
with her life savings, she started wearing that wig, going
without makeup, and wearing dull clothes. It was so nutty.
For her, I mean. It was like she had slipped into another
person's skin, kind of the way the actors in horror movies
slipped into prosthetic faces and other body parts. Yet I
knew this must have been how she looked, more or less,
back when she was growing up in Darien, Connecticut,
before she went to Princeton and fell in with a coven of
witches there.

The wig and the clothes lasted about a week. Then I
hired her to consult on our special report on the paranormal, and she reverted to herself.

"Sally, calm down. Don't jump to any conclusions. Everything will be fine," I said, putting one arm around her.

"How do you know everything will be okay?"

"I have no choice but to believe that," I said.

"Maybe if I burn some bladderwrack . . . Omigod, bladderwrack won't do it, will it? I really fucked up," Sally said.
"I'm a complete fraud. I knew it."

"Sally, don't do anything drastic. Everything is going to
be all right."

"Yeah, that's what I told your friend, that everything
would be all right, and I was wrong," Sally bawled so the
whole place could hear. I'm sure this instilled lots of confidence in people who were waiting to have their fortunes

read. "Oh God, I just had a vision flash through my head . . . a terrible vision. . . ."

"It's all some kind of joke, Sally. Don't panic. You're only human. Can you tell me anything else about this Anne, whose name is really Julie?"

"She seemed so nice. I was helping her a lot with her problems."

"What problems?"

"The married boss, the wife, and she had a bad childhood."

Julie's childhood was bad, I had to admit. But lots of people had shittier childhoods. Sooner or later, you deal with it and move on, right?

Sally couldn't stop crying. I kept rubbing her back with one hand as I whipped out my notebook with the other and started playing with the name. Anne Winston. It wasn't up to Julie's regular standards. She'd always liked aliases like Carol Merrill, Terence J. Mahoney, or Putli Bai, Indian Bandit Queen.

I studied the clue again.

"Grand," I read again. "Four Eyes cousin with leg braces."

It took me a few minutes of brain strain and a few more passes over the clue to figure it all out. Grand was the name of the best hotel in Ferrous.

Four Eyes. There was a kid, a grade ahead, nicknamed Four Eyes. Come to think of it, he had a young cousin with leg braces who attended Camp Hapalot. . . . Victor? Vincent.

There was a Hotel Vincent, near Gramercy Park, and we had stopped there, very, very briefly, that night in New York, on the ride back to our hotel.

My phone rang in my hand, startling me and scaring Sally into a more energetic round of sobbing.

"Robin? Claire. Still can't find anything on Anne Winston."

"I wonder if she's a real person, and Julie's just been using her name tonight. Hmmm. What about George the rich guy?"

Sally got up and went to the bar. Out of the corner of my eye, I saw her order and pound back a shot of something.

"Nothing yet," Claire said. "Nobody on the night shift has a fucking clue, so I'm sitting here between two computers, one doing a slow search through last week's scripts for the words 'fugitive' and 'George,' and another flashing all the newsphotos we used last week during my shows. I'll know it when I see the photo. I've only got a few dozen more to go through. Where are you going now?"

"The Hotel Vincent. I don't know why yet, but I guess I'll find out when I get there."

"I'll call you when I find out who this guy is and why he's news," Claire said. "Have you heard from Tamayo?"

"No. Wasn't she with you?"

"She went to check out the apartment building Julie Goomey lived in before 1990."

"I was just about to call her. . . ."

"I just called her, Rob. There was no answer. I'm worried. Very worried."

"She may have gone to talk to someone and left the phone somewhere. You know how absent-minded she can be."

"Robin, I have a very bad feeling about all this. Be careful, okay?"

"Sure."

Sally was at the bar talking to Greg the "warlock." I saw her put back another shot of something.

"Sally, I gotta go," I said. "Take it easy, sweetie."

"I'll go with you," she said, already slurring her words.

"No, you can't go with me. I'll call you tomorrow," I said.

"Have another drink," said the warlock.

I wanted to stay and look after Sally, but I couldn't, and I couldn't take her with me either, not in her state. Jeez, this good-friend stuff was tricky. Before I left, I called a car service to get a car to take her home. Even though it was just a few long blocks from here back to our apartment building, and traffic was going to be a pain because of all the people on the streets, I felt better having professionals take her home. There was a long wait for a car, so I took the bartender aside and asked her to keep an eye out for Sally in the interim, try to get her away from the warlock. I also left a message with the bartender for Tamayo, in case she showed up here, that I was going to the Hotel Vincent, and she should call me or Claire.

When I left the Neon Hand on Avenue A, that Yma Sumac song I'd heard at Joy II, "Virgenes del Sol," started playing in an endless loop somewhere at the back of my head—beating drums, chanting men, Yma's desperate, ethereal shriek. My heart was beating to the drums. I couldn't even feel my legs.

The megavitamin was finally kicking in.

❖ 16 ❖

ON AVENUE A, I made my way through the sea of garish
masks and painted faces—two people in big Babar heads,
a couple of skeletons, some ghosts, vampires, aliens—as
well as people not in costumes. I saw Munch's *The Scream*
walking behind me, and that gave me a start. Maybe it was
a different *The Scream*. Maybe it was an amazing coincidence.

I looked down 10th Street, my street. Beams of artificial
light glanced off the dark street, sharp as knives, from the
bright lights along the basketball-court fence. I was just a
block and a half from my bed, from safety, and it was with
a heavy heart I kept on walking towards Gramercy.

There were too many voices in my head. I felt like the
guy with the tinfoil earmuffs, trying to tune in a clear signal. I couldn't hear the voice in my own head. I heard
Julie's voice, Claire's, Old Hobnail's, Sally's, Tamayo's,
Yma Sumac's, Mary MacCosham's. . . .

I was within sight of the Vincent now. Julie and I had
stopped outside the Hotel Vincent for, maybe, five minutes
that night in 1979. Because of an unexpected detour,
caused by a minor car accident, we'd turned west in the
Gramercy Park area and gone past it. Julie, struck by it,
asked the driver to stop. It is a very impressive-looking
building, a Victorian Gothic red brick building with
wrought-iron balconies and a lot of interesting turrets and
gargoyles. We spent all of five minutes looking at it and
then, as I recall, I got cranky because I was tired and drunk
and needed some sleep. After that, I know we went back
to the Abbey Victoria. The next day, we'd looked up the

Vincent in a guidebook and learned it was a historic artists' hotel, home to a lot of famous painters over the years.

"Let's stay there next time we come to New York," Julie said. She'd said the same thing about the ritzy Hotel Delmonico up on Park Avenue, and the Plaza on Fifth, so the Vincent didn't stick with me particularly.

We didn't come back to New York together, but Julie stayed here when she came back to New York the summer of 1979 with Mary MacCosham. The Vincent must have been a walk on the wild side for her then best friend, Mary. It's a bohemian residential hotel, a refuge for tortured, semi-insane artists and the like, known variously to its residents as The Mothership, The Asylum, and, during those creatively dry times when the rent is overdue, The Dorm at Hell U.

My phone rang.

"Robin? Claire."

I could hardly hear her.

"You have to shout, Claire, I'm getting a low-battery light in my phone now. Shit. I have lousy phone karma."

"I've been trying to call you for ten minutes. I finally jumped in a cab. I'm heading down to the Hotel Vincent, Robin. Do you recognize the name Johnny 'Nostrils' Chiesa?"

"It sounds familiar. But why?"

Her voice faded in and out. ". . . don of the Perrugia family . . . the guy in the tub . . ."

"George the rich guy?"

"George is Johnny," she shouted, and began reading. "Like the Genovese family, the Perrugias resisted narcotics and pornography, reputedly concentrating on loan-sharking and protection rackets in New York's Garment District and Times Square. They claim they are in the Italian soda-import business and . . . have a successful soda business.

"Johnny . . . husband of the eldest of Gaspar and Sophia Perrugia's four daughters . . . no sons.

". . . family prospered in the 1980s, adding the Wall Street district to its loan-sharking operations. . . ."

Her voice zoned out completely at this point. I shook the phone until it came in a little clearer.

". . . crackdown on the Big Five families took a big bite out of their income, they recovered in the early 1990s by expanding their money-laundering operations. Even . . . IRS admits they can't trace . . . family's byzantine trans-actions. . . ."

"What? I can't hear you, Claire."

". . . only the since-recanted testimony of a rival Gen-ovese capo to go on."

"George or Johnny, whoever he is, why was he news this week?"

". . . to be sentenced yesterday on a weapons violation, and he disappeared . . . a fugitive . . ."

"Does it say anything about Frankie the Fish?" A Perrugia-family thug, murdered long ago, somehow figured into all this. Damn. My life had been so murder-free for so long. It made me think of these lifeguards in Florida who threw a party to celebrate their first year without a tragedy, during which party a guest fell into the pool and drowned.

"What?" She shouted.

I was thinking out loud. "And who is Granny?" I shouted.

". . . matriarch, mother of Gaspar . . . Chiesa's grand-mother-in-law."

"Why do I have a feeling Granny is our ace in the hole?"

"How so, Rob?"

"I don't know yet. We'll cross that bridge when we come

to it. Or, as the Afghans say, you're not even at the Bara River and already you're removing your trousers."

There was silence. When Claire's voice came back in, I heard, ". . . haven't heard from Tamayo. Tried calling her . . ."

"I'm losing you, Claire."

"Robin, they may have tuned in to your phone frequency . . ." she said, and then my phone went dead. I shook it a few times, but nothing happened.

If George was Johnny Nostrils, then maybe that fed was a fed. But who were the four wig-wearing women? The four daughters of Gaspar and Sophia, I thought. And they had Kathy. They knew I'd talked to that fed, so they must have been following me. I looked back, and saw a few people, no one wearing anything I recognized, no nose glasses or *The Screams* lurking about, though they may have been ducking in and out of the shadows. From now on, I had to watch what I said, what I did.

If I tried calling in the authorities now, Kathy, and maybe Tamayo, could be in danger. What to do, what to do. Claire would know what to do. I hoped.

Johnny Chiesa, fugitive—and what better night to make your escape than Halloween. He'd been at the Help for Kids office, Kathy had called there. Had he lured her up to find out why she was on his trail? Was Julie setting him up? How exactly did she figure into this? Did his wife find him there? That must have been where they grabbed Kathy. . . . Was Johnny dead in the tub, or faking his death so he could get away? Why was he running out on a bullshit weapons rap anyway, when he could do the year, be out, be back in business?

It was still sinking in. Unless I'd misunderstood Claire, George the rich guy was Johnny Nostrils, wanted mobster.

We hadn't been out with a generous, sophisticated businessman during our first trip to New York. We'd been out with a gangster. No bloody wonder people fell all over themselves to kiss our asses and give us free stuff when we walked into those designer showrooms with Johnny Nostrils. Jesus, we were so naïve.

That's why George looked familiar in that old photograph, I thought. I must have seen his picture somewhere in a mob story, and filed it away in the useless-information part of my brain. I'm not a big mob maven. My ex, Burke, was really into mob stories, but I was always more interested in stories about people who killed people they were supposed to love.

Living in New York, you can't help picking up a little of the mob news just by osmosis. I mean, I knew the big stuff, about John Gotti, and about Chin Gigante, who eluded jail for a long time by feigning madness, walking up and down Mulberry in his bathrobe and slippers muttering to himself. And, thanks to an organized-crime exhibit at the New York Historical Society, which Burke had taken me to, I knew a few historical stories about the mob—how Albert Anastasia was gunned down in a barbershop chair at the Park Sheraton, how a Murder Inc. stool pigeon, Abe "Kid Twist" Reles was put into protective custody and despite a twenty-four-hour armed guard was pushed to his death from his room at the Half Moon Hotel in Coney Island. I knew that a century ago gangs calling themselves the Plug Uglies and the Dead Rabbits roamed Five Points (the intersection of Orange, Cross, Anthony, Little Water, and Mulberry streets in what is now Little Italy/Chinatown), and that in the nineteenth century a ruffian-for-hire routinely charged $2 for a punch, $15 to bite off an ear, and $100 to kill someone.

But about contemporary mobsters I knew very little.

Just enough to know that these are not people to fuck with. Duh.

Well, there's a big difference between me and Julie, I thought. To me, "don't fool around with mobsters" is a matter of common sense. Admittedly, common sense isn't my strong point, but I'd had more of it than Julie. Julie had had a different kind of genius.

It was too bad we got so drunk the night we met the gangsters. Although, in retrospect, I don't think we had more than a half-dozen wine spritzers each in the course of the night, and we'd eaten a couple of times. Hmmm. Being older and wiser, etc., I had to wonder if George/Johnny or Billy hadn't slipped something into our drinks. When we got home, we slept eleven hours, through two wakeup calls.

Despite everything, I couldn't believe Julie would put me through all this without a very good reason. There had been bad times, sure, there had been resentments and, apparently, long-held grudges. But you grow up, a little bit, let go of some of the past, decide what you want to carry with you into the future.

There had been good times too. She had to remember those. There had been love there. And co-conspiracy. We learned a lot from each other. The first time I kissed a boy was in her basement, the first time I smoked a cigarette was with her, the first time I tasted a beer. Together, we got even with Mary MacCosham. Julie told me about sex and went with me to buy Tampax to replace the awkward Kotex belt-and-pad contraption. I could still see Julie unflinchingly taking the Tampax to the drugstore counter and paying for it, in full sight of everyone in the store. I thought that was so brave.

True, at times I was a shitty friend to Julie. I ratted her out, indirectly, to Doug Gribetz. Not only that, but I ratted

Julie out to our sewing teacher, Old Hobnail, after the wet-
ass incident. I never told Julie that either. After Hobbins
caught up with her, I let her think Hobbins had figured it
out for herself. Of course, now I realize, Hobbins did figure
it out. She detained me and accused me in order to put a
wedge between me and Julie, punish us both in a sinister
way, by making me rat Julie out.

But, damn, the statute of limitations had expired on that
too, long ago.

The Vincent loomed ahead. My legs were going towards
it, but my heart and brain were hanging back.

Every year you read a wire story about how a whole
family was killed, one right after another, by deadly, odor-
less methane gas which had built up in a closed manure
pit. In almost every one of these stories, the first person
goes in and doesn't come out, the second person wonders
where he is and goes in to see what's going on and he
doesn't come out either, so the third guy goes in . . . and
so on. Up to five people have been killed this way. You'd
think, after three guys had gone into a manure pit, not
responded to calls, not come out, the next guy would think,
"Wait a second. Maybe I shouldn't go in there. Maybe I
should get help."

I felt like the fourth guy, about to go blindly into the
manure pit.

After hours, you have to get buzzed into the Vincent, unless a man in a tuxedo ahead of you gets buzzed in first
and holds the door for you, as happened to me. The key
from the envelope Sally had given me had no tag, so I
stopped at the desk and asked the night clerk if someone
had left something for Robin Hudson. He handed me a
little piece of paper which bore only the words "Doug Gribetz's birthday"—which was July 21, 7/21—and another

from the housekeeping staff, confirming that the guest had requested no housekeeping service until the next afternoon.

I looked back casually to see if Claire had arrived. She wasn't there.

"When was this room rented, when was check-in?" I said to the clerk, who was reading a skin mag and absent-mindedly swatting flies.

The clerk looked it up. "Yesterday evening."

"Do you remember a dark-haired woman . . ."

"I wasn't working here yesterday evening," he said, in a please-leave tone of voice.

"If a woman in a dog costume comes in, or one looking like Marilyn Monroe, please tell them I'll be in 721," I said.

"Sure," he said, and went back to swatting flies.

Seven twenty-one was in a little cul-de-sac of rooms. I knocked. When there was no answer, I put the key in the lock and opened the door, shut it quickly behind me, then bolted it and chained it.

A very old woman was fast asleep in the double bed, next to an empty wheelchair.

"You must be Granny," I said softly.

On top of the dresser was a note on stationery from Metro Home Nurse, "your temporary home nurse specialists."

Dear Ms. Winston,
I have bathed, fed and given the medication you left for your grandmother. She should sleep through the night. She was very disoriented and confused and at first refused to go to bed. I did get her into bed. As per your instructions, I left at midnight. The morning nurse will be here at 6 A.M.

She gave emergency numbers and signed it "Frances Johnson, R.N."

I poked the old woman to make sure she was alive, and she snorted and fell back to sleep.

There was a flash outside the window. I looked out. A moon, partially obscured by clouds, shone between the pink neon hotel sign and a black water-tank on spindly legs on a roof across the street. Dry lightning cracked about.

Well, now I guess I wait for Claire and the cavalry. I sat down in the wheelchair and opened the envelope Julie had left for me on the desk, taking out a thick sheaf of papers. On top was a typewritten note that said, inexplicably, "Don't say I never did anything for you."

Underneath were some photocopied pages from a book called *Mob Myths: New York Mafia Legends 1925–1995*, written by a longtime *New York Post* crime reporter, and a computer printout that looked to me like a bunch of financial transactions. The computer printout was pretty meaningless to me, but I suspected it would interest the feds.

The first photocopied section from the book was the story of a mob enforcer, F., who had been assigned by a high-ranking capo in a small but powerful family to knock off another high-ranking capo in the family, J., who was married to the eldest daughter of the don. The family was undergoing a power struggle while the don, G., was on his deathbed. The intended victim, J., was tracked to a midtown bar, where he believed he'd be meeting with a colleague. The "colleague" was supposed to take him out and kill him. Unbeknownst to the "colleague," J. caught on to the plan and tried to get away through the men's room, which also opened into the hotel that housed the bar. The hit man/colleague followed him into the john and insisted on escorting J. out.

But on the way out of the john, the intended victim saw

two girls, and invited them to have drinks. He used these two nice girls from the Midwest as a shield all evening, refusing to let the hit man go and luring him, finally, to a spot where the hit man could be grabbed by two of the intended victim's henchmen. The hit man was taken off and killed, but it wasn't until a decade later that his bones were found in the Dunes in Bedford-Stuyvesant, near the old Brooklyn dump.

Jesus H. Billy was Frankie the Fish. We'd blundered into a hit that night! Fuck. Billy, or Frankie, whatever his name was, had been killed that night. Julie and I had saved Johnny Nostrils's life, and cost the other guy his. Julie had done it, really. Every time Billy suggested that he and George had to go meet some business colleagues, Julie insisted we keep going, even to the point of grabbing Billy by one arm while I grabbed the other, all of this with George's encouragement. What was Billy going to do, pull a gun on us in public?

And when we held Billy/Frankie at Cafe Buñuel, we gave Johnny Chiesa a chance to use the pay phone by the john, call his cohorts to come get Frankie the Fish.

God, we were lucky we didn't get offed along with Johnny Nostrils. The mob was bad, but they did have a code of honor that precluded the murder of innocent bystanders. Partly this was because innocent bystanders brought the swift wrath of the cops and the media, especially when said innocent bystanders are dead tourist girls. Only after most of the Mafia was broken did sloppier, more ruthless gangs move in and kids and other innocents get killed from stray bullets in gang crossfires and drive-bys.

After that excerpt was a story about Godmother G., mother of the dead don G., who was said to be the brains behind the family until a head injury resulting from a fall in 1989 left her daft. Before the head injury, she had been

the meanest woman in the Mafia, believed to be responsible
for the mysterious disappearance and presumed murder of
two women with whom her husband had long affairs. As
soon as her ailing husband slipped into a coma, the mis-
tresses vanished.

Godmother G.'s son Don G. had four daughters, the
eldest married to the man, J., who took over the family
after the Godfather died.

Shit. I looked over at Granny. She looked so sweet and
harmless now. You could hardly even tell she was a mur-
deress.

Where was Claire? I wondered if I should call the feds.
What if the room phone was tapped or something? What
if the feds showed up before I got Kathy and Tamayo back?
How would the Perrugia sisters call me now that my cell
phone was dead? I looked for the room phone. There was
none. Someone had removed it.

Granny was snoring loudly away. In between snores, I
heard pounding at the door. Quietly, I crept to the peephole, looked out, and saw someone in one of those cheap,
over-the-head skeleton costumes.

"Who are you?" I said. "Show your face."

Two delicate hands rose, with identical movements, and
pulled the front of the costume up over the top of her
head.

It was Mary MacCosham, and did she looked pissed.
More than pissed. She was wild-eyed, like she was manic,
or on something. Evidently, Mary had gone off the deep
end.

"Open this damn door," she said. "Or I'll shoot it
open."

⊗ 17 ⊗

IN THE MOMENT before I opened the door, there was, like, an atomic explosion in my head.

Mary's middle name was Anne. Her mother's maiden name was something like Winston. Anne Winston. I don't know why I didn't think of it before. I guess I was thinking in a different groove.

Mary was involved with charity. Mary had tried to buy her way up through society with charity fund-raising work. She seemed the type to have tasteful Park Avenue decor. Hell, she was a Park Avenue trophy wife, in a small-time way, until her divorce.

Not only that, but she'd come back to New York with Julie—she no doubt knew a lot about our itinerary. Had she and Julie hooked up with George when they were here? Maybe that photo of Julie and George was taken during their trip. Maybe they'd gone to some of the same places.

Shit, yes! The handwritten note from Julie that was included with the cootie catcher I was given at Joy II was dated August 7, 1979, after our falling out. Apparently, it was a note to Mary MacCosham.

That explained the lame alias.

But why was she fucking with me? Was this part of her motherfucker of a midlife crisis? Some settling of old scores?

So—where was Julie? Hell. I'd been chasing her all night, and she was probably a happily remarried housewife in New Mexico, asleep in her bed tonight, ignorant of all this.

Boy, I had to give Mary credit. Mary was a little cleverer than I had imagined, not as clever as Julie, but pretty clever.

I didn't have any weaponry with me. I tried to pick up the lamp on the bedside table, but it was bolted down. There was nothing, so I just opened the door, and, going purely on instinct, popped Mary right in the nose, three times, very quickly.

"This one is for me, this one is for Julie, and this one is for making Mabel eat her own Barbie," I said. This was the rare instance where a punch in the nose was better than a sturdy Anglo-Saxon word.

Mary MacCosham dropped to the floor.

Somewhere, doors were opening.

I pulled Mary's body into the room and slammed the door.

She was out, but not dead. Thank God. The last thing I needed now was a dead crazy socialite mob moll on my hands. At her side was a gun, but a toy, not a real one. Quickly, I dumped her purse out. Among the contents were expensive cosmetics, a bottle of Midol, a handkerchief, which I placed over Mary's bleeding nose, a brown envelope folded in half and containing what looked like a lot of money, a vial of what looked like coke, and a typed letter.

It was the second page of a note—or made up to look that way, with the number 2 up in the corner—that read:

> photos. As you know, these photos could ruin your chance to regain custody of your kids. If you want them back, go to the Hotel Vincent, and wait for the redhead in 721. Bring $10,000 in unmarked bills. Go to the cops and it's over for you.

It was signed "Putli Bai."

That fucking Julie had set us both up. Julie tricked me with those Mary MacCosham clues. Or had I just jumped to the wrong conclusion, because of her nice furniture, when I saw Mary at the door? Or all of the above? Julie must have faked the note dated after our falling out, then thrown in the photo with the September date, and the lame alias to lead me astray. If only Rubik had known Julie.

There were no photos for Mary among the things Julie had left here, so I assumed Julie had totally faked Mary out with that bit. Maybe she knew something about Mary, maybe she didn't. Knowing Mary's weak points, she could have pushed her buttons very easily by bluffing.

I filled a paper cup with water from the tap and dumped it on Mary. She moaned a little, but didn't come to. I shook her slightly and her eyes opened.

"Aieaie . . . ooooh," she moaned.

"Long time no see, Mary," I said.

She tried to get up but couldn't.

"Sorry I had to bean you. I misunderstood."

"Do you have the photos?"

"As far as I know, there are no photos."

"No . . . but . . . Who are you? You look vaguely familiar."

"Robin, Robin Hudson."

"Robin?"

"Yeah, Mary."

She held the handkerchief over her bleeding nose and said, weakly, "Who's the old woman?"

"It's a long story. Julie Goomey set us up," I said, and I gave her the capsule version while I flushed her coke. I was expecting Claire any minute, possibly with cops, and I didn't want Mary getting busted on a possession rap. I had a feeling she'd been through enough.

When I was finished, all Mary could say was, "Why? What did I ever do to her?"

"Whatever," I said. "Listen, are you okay now? Can you get up? Because I need you to help me."

I held my hand out to her and she grabbed it, hoisting herself to her knees. When she'd stabilized, she pulled herself to her feet.

I gave her Special Agent Jeff Walter's card. "Call this guy. Tell him where I am. Tell him—this is very important, let me write it down." I wrote a short note, explaining that the Perrugia sisters were holding my intern and my friend hostage, that I had their granny and I needed to effect an exchange discreetly so nothing would happen to Kathy and Tamayo. I put down my room number.

"After you make this call, go to the front desk and tell them the phone is missing in this room and I need a phone immediately."

"I don't know," Mary said. She was looking at me with deep suspicion. "How do I know this isn't one of your jokes?"

"Why would I do that?"

"Why did you send the Dumpster salesmen to my house? Or write the letters at Camp Hapalot? Or send me on all those wild-goose chases?"

"I didn't. Okay, I sent the Dumpster salesmen to your house—that was my idea—but those other things were Julie's ideas, not mine."

"Really? Because a long time ago Julie told me . . . she blamed you . . ."

She was still groggy.

"Just call this guy, please," I said. "He probably knows a lot of stuff I don't know and he can explain it better. Just do it. Lives are at stake. No shit."

After she picked up her purse, with none of the urgency I wanted her to display, she turned to me, and said, "Why did you flush my coke?"

"Please call this guy."

Mary just looked at me. Then she left. I hoped I could trust her.

I sat down. The voices in my head were all clamoring for attention. I held my head between my hands, thinking maybe, if I just steadied my head, the right voice would squeeze through. Somehow, I had to make contact with the Groucho women. Before I could figure out how, there was another knock at the door. I looked out the peephole and saw a big dog-face staring back at me.

"Good timing!" I said, quickly unlocking the door so she could slip in without whoever else seeing her. "Claire, jeez, what took ya. You will never believe . . ."

Immediately I realized what was wrong. But immediately was too late. There was a gun in my chest. Jojo the Health and Safety Dog backed me into the room and the door slammed behind us.

The dog head came off. Underneath was a pretty, dark-haired woman with a very unpleasant expression on her face. She put down a drawstring bag, which fell open to reveal a green wig, Groucho-nose glasses, and what looked like a mask of some kind. I couldn't tell what it was, but I guessed that she had changed masks at some point, or gone unmasked, to avoid detection while following me.

"Expecting me? Sorry for the delay. I ran into a big dog," she said. I recognized her voice. It was the head wig-wearing woman. "Give me your purse."

I did. She opened it, saw nothing of value, and threw it into the far corner, out of my reach.

After glancing at the documents Julie had left, she scooped them up into her bag.

"Sit down over there," she said, walking backwards towards the old woman.

She poked the old woman. "Granny, wake up."

The woman just snorted and fell back to sleep.

"She's out. She was given something," I said. "There's a note on the dresser."

"Uh-huh," she said. She picked it up and handed it to me.

"Read it to me," she said.

I did.

"Where's Julie?" she said.

"I don't know. Rio, probably. But you have your granny and you have those documents. I think I've lived up to my end of the bargain."

"Yeah, whatever," the woman said. She pulled out a cell phone and dialed carefully, pushing a number, looking up at me, pushing another one, looking up at me again.

"Hello? It's me. I've got them, Granny, the redhead, and a whole pile of spread sheets."

A beat.

"No, she's not here. I don't know if we'll get the money back. Well, what did you expect? At least we have Granny and the documents. Maybe we can recover some of the money."

Pause.

"I'd rather not kill anyone here unless I have to. I had to ask the clerk for the room number, so I've been seen. You want me to leave a body here? Besides, this isn't a very good silencer."

Kill anyone? Jeez. She was talking about me. Where were the fucking feds?

"Get Granny's van and then get right over here. It's the Hotel Vincent. We'll take them out together. How long will it take you? Okay. We'll be down in front in fifteen minutes. Don't make me wait too long. And send the boys to pick up a blonde in the utility closet on the seventh floor. I knocked her out."

That had to be Mary. Knocked out twice in one night. Damn. Now she wouldn't be able to call Special Agent Jeff Walter.

A pause.

"She's fast asleep but otherwise she seems okay. Julie had the decency to hire a nurse to look after her until midnight. Okay. Right. Okay."

She hung up.

"Where's Claire?" I asked.

"Which one is that?"

"The black woman?"

"We got her outside the hotel. One of my sisters took her. You think we didn't see you with her? We got the Chinese girl outside Neon Hand. . . . We grabbed the bald woman there too. And now we have your blond friend. That's what you get for being mixed up with Julie Goomey."

"They weren't mixed up with her. They don't even know her. And I didn't want to be mixed up with her," I said. "I haven't seen the woman in almost two decades."

"Tough titty," she said.

Okay, I was thinking, she's a woman. Maybe I can access that empathy thing, meet her on that nurturing, sisterhood plane that women are supposed to have biologically. She loves her granny, how bad can she be? I was willing to bet she even laughed at quality fart jokes and had a few legendary Girls' Nights Out under her belt.

"You know, I'm an innocent bystander. I don't wish you or yours any harm, I just want me and my friends to get out of this alive," I said.

"You know too much, princess," she said.

"I'm not a princess."

"Oh, come on. I know girls like you and Julie. Country clubs, trust funds, college, think your shit doesn't stink."

"I did go to college, but otherwise you are way off."

"Well, I went to college too," she said, defensively.

"I didn't come from money and I had a crappy childhood, no country clubs, my dad died when I was ten. . . ."

Now I was trying a strategy my Southern friend Carol calls "Don't kick the cripple," to make her feel guilty for picking on me. It was something I'd seen Solange do.

"Cry me a river," she said. "You try being the eldest of four sisters living in a fucking compound in New Jersey. Every inch of your life is controlled."

"I'm sorry," I said, trying to express some genuine empathy. It was a bad move.

"Don't you feel sorry for me, princess," she said, gesticulating with the gun. "Feel sorry for yourself."

"Did you have cooties?" I ventured weakly.

"You're the one with the fucking cooties!"

Okay, we weren't going to bond that way. I decided to attempt another tried-and-true bonding technique, the enemy-of-my enemy strategy.

"Julie Goomey is a bitch," I said. "She really fucked me over, and my friends too. We're in the same boat."

"No, we're not. I have the gun. You think I don't know that she's been fucking with all of us? She let us know, in her special little way, that Johnny was hiding out on Park Avenue. That's how we found the girl hiding in the closet, got the tip about the strip joint, and started tracking you."

"Don't you folks adhere to a code wherein you don't kill innocent bystanders?"

"You're not so innocent, princess," she said.

That's when I remembered this other mob story I read, out of Italy. The authorities there thought they'd broken the back of the Sicilian Mafia when they jailed all the top men. But they didn't bank on the women of the families, who took over, and were even more ruthless than the men. No longer were other women and children safe in vendettas. Makes ya think.

"What do you know about Julie?" I said. "I mean, I haven't seen her in a long time. Why was she fucking with everyone this way?"

"She's been screwing my bastard husband for the last five or six years, that we know. She's been running our financial operations for almost as long, though we didn't know that until Johnny was about to go to jail. She was supposed to turn over control to us, but she disappeared and Granny vanished from the hospital. It's been a shitty couple of days, and on top of everything else, I'm fucking premenstrual. So don't give me a hard time."

She looked at her watch. "It's time to go. You're gonna have to push Granny's wheelchair."

She took out two pairs of handcuffs and ordered me to put her granny in the wheelchair.

The woman, dead to the world, weighed a ton. It was like trying to manipulate a ninety-pound sack of cooked oatmeal. At one point, I accidentally swung Granny, and her hand went flying, smacking me in the face. That gave me an idea.

I swung Granny a couple more times to get her arms moving, and then, suddenly, I smacked the gun out of the Perrugia woman's hand with Granny's left hand. It fell to the floor and she went for it. I followed her, and when she tried to cut me off, I beat her some more with her own granny, smacking her upside the head.

The woman dodged. Granny faked her out with her right and then slapped her with her left.

"Stop that!" the Perrugia sister said.

Granny slapped her again. She was inches from the gun when I dumped her granny on top of her and made a break for the weapon.

Her hand reached it a half-inch before mine.

"Stop right there!" She pointed the gun at me, and gently shoved her granny aside.

"Now you're really in for it. Now I'm going to hurt you bad," she said. "You're going to die slow tonight. One of my cousins has a meatpacking plant. How'd you like to go through the hamburger grinder alive instead of dead?"

"I wouldn't," I said, weakly.

"Too late. Now, get Granny into that wheelchair."

I wrestled her into the chair.

"Put your hands on the handles."

After she cuffed me to the chair, she threw a blanket over her grandmother's shoulders to cover my cuffs, and fastened Granny's seatbelt.

"Let's go. Don't make any more trouble. I'm sure you're smart enough to know that."

Yeah, I'm a smart girl. After the fact.

I'm going to die, I thought. I've thought this more than once, from times I've had guns on me, all too often, to my last bout with stomach flu when I was sure I'd picked up some weird life-threatening virus from a trip to the rain forest with Mike. But this time, I couldn't see a way out of it. I started to cry.

"Can the waterworks, princess," the woman says. "Or it'll be worse."

I was having a hard time regaining control. Another sob

escaped. My tears moved her not a bit, just made her angrier.

"Get control. Or I will make your friends suffer before I kill them too."

I closed my eyes. I sucked back the tears. I calmed myself.

❖ 18 ❖

I PUSHED GRANNY out of the room while Mrs. Johnny Chiesa followed close behind. The thirty or so feet to the elevator was the longest thirty feet of my life. When the elevator arrived it was pretty crowded, with a bunch of people who seemed to know each other, probably coming from the same soirée. Carefully, I backed in with the wheelchair, so I was jammed right up against some zonked-out party kid with bleached blond hair and thirty-seven earrings in his face. The head woman slid in beside me and the doors closed. We rode down a couple of floors and stopped; the doors opened again, producing a breeze. A man in a paint-covered shirt got on.

All I could think was, I'm going to die, and none of these festive strangers know it. This was the only audible voice in my head now. Normally, at this moment, what would pass before my eyes is not my past but my made-up past. Because, when I die, a very special fake obit my friend Louis Levin and I put together will air, and ANN's worldwide viewers will see me Forrest Gump–style, in a number of historical moments. Me, in slinky red dress and high heels, at the Battle of the Bulge, during Nixon's trip to China, waiting on the moon with a Hawaiian lei to greet Neil Armstrong when he takes his giant leap for mankind. There's me on the arm of playwright-actor Sam Shepard, on my way to Scandinavia to pick up my Nobel prizes for both peace and literature. In our last update, we had added a few testimonials from celebrities and regular folks, culled from infomercials, so that Cher and Victoria Principal thanked me for solving their hair-care problems, an Illinois

autoworker credited me for relieving his male itch, and a
bunch of nice retired couples sang my praises for teaching
them how to buy real estate with no money down. And at
the end, there are thousands of grief-stricken North Ko-
reans prostrate before giant pictures of me in Pyongyang.

But this time, my past, made up or otherwise, didn't
flash before my eyes. My future did, or, rather, the future
I could be losing out on, and what I saw was me with
Mike, and me alone in some strange place, and me with
my girlfriends in thirty years, a bunch of laughing old
women pinching young Italian guys' asses while on vacation in Rome.

The door opened at the lobby, and I had started to leave
when I heard, "Yut Ya Yah."

"He's stuck on your hair," said a guy with black eyeliner
and fangs.

I tried to turn around to see but couldn't. There was a
shriek of pain.

"Careful, careful," said the man with fangs. We all
moved out of the elevator en masse. The Perrugia woman
went to the desk and said, "Do you have any scissors? This
boy is stuck to my friend."

In the mirror on the far wall, I could see that the kid
with thirty-seven earrings in his face was stuck to the back
of my head. Somehow, my corkscrew hair and his earrings
had bonded to produce a Velcro effect.

While the clerk at the desk looked for scissors, the guy
with the fangs was walking out with his boyfriend, laughing. It hit me then: The wig-wearing women are going to
turn me into hamburger. I'm going to become someone's
burger. I could end up in the school lunch program! And
not just me, my friends. No matter what I do now, they're
going to kill us.

But . . . I had a shield on the front and the back. Just

the way Frankie the Fish couldn't shoot Johnny Nostrils, she ain't gonna shoot me now. We're in public—and I have her granny.

"You're going to have to come with me," I whispered to the earring-faced boy. "Hang on."

Then, as the man with fangs and his boyfriend were opening the glass doors to leave the hotel, I took off.

"Hold the door!" I shouted, running with the wheel-chair. Earring Boy was screaming, but after a short and painful lag, his survival instinct kicked in and he ran to keep up with me. The guy with fangs held the door. The Perrugia woman was shouting, "Wait, stop!"

"Check the seventh-floor utility closet!" I screamed, as we sailed through the doors.

I turned quickly onto the pavement, without thinking, and headed east, towards First Avenue. The earring guy was half piggybacked on me, screaming. The wheelchair was picking up momentum. I leaned forward, and Earring Boy leaned with me. I put my feet on the bar at the back of the chair, throwing my weight and that of the boy forward to give us thrust and keep us from falling over backwards. Granny's unconscious head swung back and forth, from side to side.

Down 21st Street we rolled, scattering a small group of late-night diners near First Avenue. I could hear the Perrugia woman hollering after me.

At the corner of First, I leaned to the right, after announcing my attentions to the kid stuck to the back of my head, who was now fully piggybacked. Granny's wheelchair took the turn on one wheel. We had made it to 20th Street when the chair hit a rock and we all tipped over.

"Yai yai yai," screamed the earring kid as we collapsed in a heap. I tried to get us both up, but it wasn't possible with my hands cuffed to the now empty wheelchair.

"Stop right . . . there," said JoJo the Health and Safety Dog, huffing and puffing. She was about ten yards behind us, with her gun in one hand and a pair of scissors in the other. She put the gun and the scissors down in order to get us and the wheelchair back up and Granny back into it, but that didn't do me much good, being handcuffed and all.

"Now I'm gonna have to kill this kid too," she said. "Sorry, kid."

I felt the weeping boy attached to me reach into his jacket pocket. He pulled something out. I saw a flash of black, and there was a gun to the head of Granny.

"Ya ya ya," he said.

"I think he's saying that you're not going to kill him, and if you don't give him the gun, he's going to shoot your Granny," I translated through huffs and puffs.

"Ya ya ya."

"He says you should give him your gun."

She hesitated.

"Ya ya ya."

"Do it now, or Granny gets it."

She did it.

"Ya ya ya."

"Now unlock my handcuffs."

She did.

"Give me her gun," I said to the young man. "And you can cut yourself free."

He took the scissors from JoJo the Health and Safety Dog and very carefully freed himself.

"Wha ya fyuck izh zhizh awout?" he said. His mouth was pretty torn up and bloody. There were tufts of red hair sticking out from every one of his bloody earrings.

Before I could answer, he said, "I'm going yo frow up," and he leaned into the gutter and vomited. I counted my small blessings then, that he'd waited until he was freed from the back of my head before he threw up.

I handcuffed the Perrugia sister to the wheelchair and took her cell phone.

"What's your sisters' number?" I said.

She gave it to me and I dialed. The earring boy started walking weakly away, cursing, in the direction of Bellevue Hospital.

"Sorry!" I said, but he didn't respond.

"Yeah?" said the voice that answered the phone.

"There's been a change of plans," I said. "I have your granny, I have your sister, and I have the gun. So what are we going to do now?"

It was completely deserted under the elevated overpass between Asser Levy Place and the East River. Even the hookers who worked this area had gone to bed for the night. There was only the faintest breeze. A piece of paper blew slow-motion down the street. I could hear the roar of traffic rising and falling from the FDR, and stranger roars coming from the drains in the gutters. A car alarm went off a few blocks away.

"I've been tampered with, I've been tampered with," the car alarm said, over and over. I made a note to get myself one and hang it around my neck from now on.

Granny was still out like a light.

A van turned off 23rd Street and slowly approached, stopped right across the street. The doors opened. I put the gun to Granny's head. Two women got out of the front, and then they pulled my friends, their hands tied, out of the van.

"Come here," I said. "Slowly."

When they got to the middle of the street, I said, "Stop right there."

They stopped.

"Drop your guns."

There was no motion. I think they thought I was bluffing, maybe that I was too much of a "princess" to shoot someone.

"Don't fuck with me," I said, pulling Granny's head up by the hair. "I'll shoot her. Hey, she's had a long, full life. So I want to see your guns on the ground."

There were guns on the ground. It made me feel a little safer, though I was sure they had some weapons in reserve.

"We want to see Granny and Wanda," said one of the women.

"Walk out five steps," I said to JoJo the Health and Safety Dog. I pushed Granny just barely into the light. I still had the gun to her head.

"Let my friends go," I said.

They released my friends. Sally was staggering and had to lean against Claire for support. She looked bad. They walked past me and sat down on a patch of grass in Asser Levy Place.

"Wanda, take Granny. The documents you want are in her lap," I said.

The Perrugia sisters ran forward, grabbing Granny and Jojo. Suddenly, two more women jumped out of the van, followed by two men, all with guns drawn, and came towards me. We appeared to be massively outgunned.

That's when JoJo's head came off.

"You are under arrest," said Special Agent Jeff Walter, half man, half Safety Dog. He started reading the Miranda, a bunch of feds appeared, and a bright light suddenly shone down the street.

Hey, I'm not *that* stupid. The first thing I did after I got off the phone with the Mafia queen was call the feds from the nearest untraceable pay phone. It was my card to play—I had Granny and Mrs. Johnny Chiesa. The next thing I did was, I called the All News Network and got a crew down here.

Granny was still asleep. One of the cops wheeled her away. Bellevue was just around the corner—she'd be taken there and checked out, to make sure she was, more or less, okay. I felt a bit bad for her, really I did, putting her in jeopardy the way I had. But, hey, if it's a choice between her or me, I choose me.

☼ 19 ☼

"SALLY IS IN BAD SHAPE," Claire said. "One of the feds and I are going to take her to the hospital."

Tamayo went with one car of feds, Kathy and I went with another, while a police van carted away the cuffed Perrugia sisters and the ANN crew took the tape back to the network.

In the car, I hugged Kathy so hard she said, "Robin, you're hurting me."

"I'm just so glad you're alive. I am so sorry you got sucked into this."

"I thought it was a joke at first," she said. "Until they pulled the gun on me."

As I suspected, Kathy had been lured up to Julie's safe house on Park Avenue, aka Help for Kids, by Johnny, who told her that he worked for the organization and that I'd already called and was on my way. Though Kathy was made a bit suspicious by his "nervous" demeanor, she went because she figured a friend of mine was involved in it.

"Yeah, that's what I figured too," I told her.

When she got there, he gave her a soft drink and asked her a lot of questions about this murder mystery, and it became clear to her that he didn't know about it. He wanted to know if she knew where Julie was, because Julie was supposed to meet him there and he'd been waiting all day for her. Just as Kathy was about to bolt, someone came in. She heard a woman's voice, and Johnny shoved Kathy into the closet. There was arguing in the other room, and Kathy pulled the phone in, "quiet as a mouse," and called the only number of mine she knew by heart, my work number, so I wouldn't worry if she didn't show up at the giant coffee cup.

Wouldn't worry. Jesus H.

"Robin, they were arguing about this Julie, and how this guy, Johnny, had taken off, abandoned her, his wife, and someone had drained all the family accounts or something. He tried to calm her down, and she asked where the wine was. When she went to get it, he whispered something to me, but I couldn't make out what he was saying.

"Then the wife came back, and they drank wine and talked in calmer tones, and suddenly there was a thump. Johnny was on the floor right outside the closet! I looked out a crack in the closet, and saw one of his big eyes staring back at me. That's when the wife found me and took me away at gunpoint."

She was trying to sound brave, but tears were streaming down her face.

"You done good, Kathy. You're a trooper. I'm sorry. . . ."

"Now that it's over," she said, wiping her eyes, "and we're safe, it seems kind of . . . exciting, you know?"

"Yeah, I know. With that attitude, you'll probably make a great reporter one day."

"You think?" she said.

"Yeah. God, I am so glad I don't have to call your mom and tell her I lost you," I said.

She smiled a little.

I was exhausted and felt strangely deflated. I know I should have been happy it was over and we were all alive, but I just felt depressed and disillusioned and tired. As we drove downtown to Federal Plaza, I looked up at all the big beautiful buildings around me and, it was funny, it all looked so strange to me.

We gave our statements. Special Agent Jeff Walter told me that Julie had worked her way up from being Johnny's

mistress and bagman to money-laundering, advancing to
run a complicated money-laundering system, using byzantine money transfers and currency exchanges, and funnel-
ing money through a series of offshore accounts. Given
Julie's demonstrated skills in leading people astray, I could
see why she was such a good money-launderer.

Among other crimes, there was major income-tax eva-
sion involved. The government wanted to jail Johnny for
a long time, and they wanted to get their hands on that
money. Julie was the key to all of it. Only she knew the
money trails. This was how she kept herself alive within
the family.

With Johnny going to jail for a year, Julie would have
to report to Johnny's wife, and Johnny's wife would just
as soon kill Julie as look at her. But first Johnny's wife
needed to learn where Julie and Johnny had stashed all the
cash.

It looked like Julie had arranged to run off with Johnny,
only she left him in the lurch, took off with all the money.
Before she vanished, she sent the FedExes out, grabbed
Granny at the convalescent hospital, and dumped her in
the Hotel Vincent. She'd left clues so the Perrugia sisters
would find Johnny at Help for Kids, and so Mary Mac-
Cosham would find me, and she'd told the feds to contact
me. I was the pawn, the wild goose. But a wild goose with
an insurance policy—Granny. And while we were running
all over Manhattan, Julie had, as far as we all knew, taken
off for points unknown.

"She's got the whole family in jail now, she's got the
money, and you've got a story. Pretty clever woman," Special Agent Jeff Walter said.

He was pretty cute, this Special Agent Jeff Walter,
Tibetan-brother cute. Very upright, clean-cut. Looked like
Dudley Do-Right, the kind of guy you just want to get real

dirty with, the kind of guy you want to corrupt a little. That's a great aphrodisiac, a man who will compromise his morals to sleep with you.

But no, it ain't gonna happen, I thought. The timing wasn't right, and I didn't expect it ever would be. But maybe, somewhere in a parallel universe . . .

"Where do you think she's gone?" he asked.

"You know, if I had any idea, I'm not sure I could tell you. Would that be breaking the law?"

"Only under oath."

"Well, I don't think she'd tell me," I said.

After we were all released, Tamayo asked, "Do you have any other pissed-off ex-friends lurking in the wings?"

"God, I hope not," I said. "I'm really sorry about this, goils. Really sorry."

I apologized all the way back to ANN, where we worked until 5 A.M. putting together the story for Claire to voice-over.

Tamayo seemed thrilled by it all, and that was rubbing off on Kathy. "It was exciting, now that it's over and everything," Tamayo said.

"You know what Carrie Fisher says, good anecdote, bad reality," I said.

The phone rang. It was someone from the assignment desk, saying there were a lot of calls from other news organizations who wanted to talk to us.

"This could be great publicity for my career," Tamayo said. "Robin, can we call a press conference?"

"Go ahead. But I'll pass, I think. Just read off the statement I gave to the assignment desk."

"I should call my agent too. Start negotiating the film rights," Tamayo said.

Tamayo and Kathy went to the outer office and started

making phone calls. And why not? Might as well make lemonade out of these lemons.

Tamayo, what a dame. It wasn't hard to see Tamayo as a playground pariah. She just grooved to her own rhythms, and if people objected, they were in need of an "anal stick-ectomy," in her words. Case closed.

Claire walked in.

We hugged and she said, "I left the report in playback, Robin. Did you call the hospital?"

"Yeah. Sally's in really bad shape. But the doctors think she'll be okay after they pump her stomach. Good thing I told them about the PMS medication she was taking on top of everything else. It turns out the PMS pills react badly with street roofies."

"Let's send her some flowers for her recovery. Poor Sal," Claire said.

"We're calling a press conference," Tamayo called out. "Want to take part?"

"No," Claire said. "I'm not interested. But you guys have fun." She turned to me. "It is fucking dangerous being your friend. But, you know, that was great, Robin. We tracked a story together, you and me, just like the old days."

"The old days."

"We broke the Perrugia family. You and me, and Tamayo, and Kathy and . . . Julie Goomey. I saw it so clearly, after the feds came, a flash in my mind. This is what your life is about, that flash said. Not being a congressman's wife, not being an anchorwoman, but being in the field, tracking a story. God, it was exhilarating, Rob. Fuck a duck."

"Did I mention that you're swearing a lot these days?"

"Bad companions," she said, turning the volume up on

the monitor in my office to hear her story about us and the Perrugia sisters.

I walked into the outer office. I just felt so strange. I looked at myself in the glass wall of a darkened office. Staring back at me was a tall, gangly girl with pale skin and frizzy red hair. It was a ghost, a cootie-girl ghost, floating in the dark glass like a character in a nightmare. That wasn't what I looked like. Where was the Rita Hayworth face that always stared back at me?

I started wondering how many other people had been murdered around me without my even being aware of it. Maybe, if I had been, I could have provided some clue. I was under a curse, just like the cab driver who couldn't escape bad traffic and was losing his penis. In addition to the curse of cooties, delivered upon my head by Mary MacCosham, people I was somehow connected to got murdered and I was menaced by wig-wearing women.

I wondered about people who died in "accidents" too. Like the guy who lived in a shack down by the railroad tracks who killed his wife while he was cleaning his gun. And all those people who died in gun-cleaning accidents in my hometown the year the iron-skillet factory closed. I remember thinking at the time that those poor people were just really stupid—I mean, why didn't they take the bullets out of their guns before they cleaned them? Duh.

But now I see.

It seemed to me that nothing was what I thought it was.

Claire came out. "You okay, Robin?"

"I don't know. Everything is upside down. And I feel responsible for everything that happened."

"You're not."

"I know this wouldn't have happened if I hadn't ratted Julie out to Lance, who ratted her out to Doug after she cheated on him in Minneapolis. She got mixed up with hoodlums, in trouble with the feds, and was going through midlife stuff, thinking how she could have been happy with Doug Gribetz if it wasn't for Robin Hudson."

"Come on, the girl has some serious psychological problems."

"She had a hard life."

"Who didn't? I had cooties too, you know?"

"*You* had cooties?"

"Well, duh. My father is black, my mother is white and Native American, it was the deep South, I was bussed, people burned a cross on our lawn once. But I survived."

"You come from a good, strong family," I said. "Julie didn't."

"So you were in love with the same boy and you pulled a nasty on her. All's fair in love and war, especially at that age. Although at least in war they have the Geneva Conventions."

"I wanted to get even with her because . . . I was jealous," I said. "I kinda liked the guy in Minneapolis Julie made out with. I mean, she had the best guy of all back home, Doug, and I felt it was unfair of her to move in on a guy I could have maybe had a shot with. But, first and foremost, I did it because I was in such puppy love with Doug, because I was jealous of her being Doug's girlfriend, and because of that joke she played on me, the letter in the locker. What if he was the guy who would have made her happy? And I fucked it up for her, my best friend. Not only that, but I knew what I was doing. I knew it was wrong."

"First of all," Claire said, "this is not a good reason to pull this kind of dangerous shit on you. What a lot of fucking nerve she has. There is no excuse. Second, are you absolutely positive that your bestest friend, Julie, wrote that letter that was stuck in your locker?"

Hmmm.

"She took the rap for it. Why would she do that if . . . No, it's not possible. Doug Gribetz knew me during my worst cootie years, and I hadn't become semipopular yet. He wouldn't have written me a love letter."

"Robin, call him," Claire said. "Or else I will."

She did too. She called directory assistance in Minneapolis, where Doug Gribetz lived. Then she dialed his number and handed me the phone.

"I'm going to go peek in on Tamayo and Kathy. Just come down when you're through, okay?" Claire said.

The phone rang seven times before a sleepy female voice answered.

"Hello?" she said.

"Is Doug there?" I asked, feeling shitty a few hundred different ways.

"May I ask who is calling?" she said, kindly.

"Robin Hudson," I said. My heart was beating inside me in time to Yma Sumac.

"Just a moment."

There was some mumbling in the background, and then I heard another voice I hadn't heard in years. Even after all these years, that voice made me melt.

"Robin," Doug said. "It's, uh, nice to hear from you. Why are you calling?"

He didn't say "at this hour." He didn't have to.

"This is an odd request, Doug. I am so sorry to disturb you." I could hear a baby crying in the background.

"It's okay. What is it?"

"Okay." I took a deep breath. "I need to know if you wrote me a letter in tenth grade and stuck it in my locker. I know this is bizarre. . . ."

"I understand . . . I guess," he said. There was a beat. "Yeah, I wrote you a letter. I thought you knew. It seems to me . . . Yeah, your friend Julie came up to me and told me that you'd read the letter and sent her to tell me that you weren't interested. So I assumed . . ."

"My friend Julie."

"Yeah. It was a long time ago, Robin. What does it matter now?"

Normally, that would be a very good question. "It's a long story, Doug."

I heard a little girl's voice say, "Daddy? The phone woke me up."

"Just a second, honey, Daddy will tuck you back in," he said.

"Well, thanks, Doug," I said. "Really sorry to bother you. Really, really sorry."

"It's okay. Take care of yourself, Robin."

"You too."

I hung up. He sounded so sweet, and his family sounded sweet. But now he was just a faraway voice on a phone, someone I didn't really know. I closed my eyes and saw his iconic face, which had remained so firmly and vividly fixed in my mind all these years, falling backwards into space, receding into a dot, and disappearing.

The same thing then happened with Julie's face. Different Julies at different ages flashed through my head, like a slide show in reverse chronological order—in the community-college quad putting up posters for pep rallies and dances, in her prom dress, slow-dancing with Doug Gribetz, in Minneapolis when we were fourteen and went down to the big city by ourselves for the first time together, in her Girl Scout uniform before we quit Girl Scouts, standing on a pier, laughing, in a bathing suit that matched mine. I saw her grow backwards from a beautiful young woman to a gangly adolescent to a cootie girl with braces and dorky cat's-eye glasses, and then to a dot, a spark

really, and then nothing. I pulled a photo out of my recovered purse and looked at it, but it was like looking at
a stranger.

I looked at my reflection again. I felt like the cab driver
with the curse, whose face was changing into someone
else's, or like one of those Oliver Sacks people who suffer
brain damage in the part of the brain that recognizes
faces, and afterwards don't recognize any face, not even
their own.

That's when the voice sounded in my head again, only
this time it was very specific.

You have to go to Two Joes, it said, sudden but quiet.

⚔ 20 ⚔

Two Joes was a classic New York coffee shop, not to be confused with the ubiquitous tony coffee bars that have mushroomed across the land. Two Joes had a half-dozen six-seater booths and a lunch counter. The humble doughnuts were kept elegantly under glass on plates atop metal stems, and in every booth one of those miniature jukeboxes perched on the wall above the square steel napkin-dispenser on the table. The waiters had potbellies barely held in by big white aprons and used their own corny code. Like, if you ordered a ham on rye, toasted, they'd ask for a "Ham on whiskey, down." Over the years, they'd used the same plain white china, unadorned except for a single rust-colored stripe just below the rim. You had to bring your own beer and wine; they weren't licensed to sell it. The last time I was there, there wasn't a fern, pastel, or faux Art Deco accent in sight. Through many changing restaurant fashions, Two Joes had remained true to its roots.

"And why is this important?" Claire asked. Out of the corner of my eye, I could see her and Tamayo exchanging indulgent, meaningful looks. Kathy had gone home.

"It's the very first place I went in Manhattan. Seeing it will help. I know it will."

It was raining that night, the evening we landed at JFK. Julie and I had taken the JFK express from the airport, but we made a mistake and got off at 34th Street instead of Rockefeller Center. There were no cabs available, but we were young, healthy women, so we began the Long March uptown, dragging our suitcases behind us. After about three blocks, the torrential rain was too much for us, so we ducked into Two Joes to wait out the storm.

One of the things I loved about Two Joes was that the first time I was there I had a moment of déjà vu. As my super, Phil, says, "You never really feel at home in a place until you experience déjà vu there," and I knew exactly what he meant. That's the thrill I was looking for tonight. That old déjà vu.

I remember the guy behind the counter, Joe, singing a song he made up about me and Julie, interrupting himself to curse at the delivery guy: "Harry, where the fuck you been you're an hour late goddammit we got orders waitin'."

Joe, he cursed at Harry not with anger, but in a matter-of-fact sort of way. Better a sturdy Anglo-Saxon word that has stood the test of time than a punch in the face, I almost always say—or, for that matter, than a stiletto to the heart.

"You're giving these girls from Minnesota a bad impression of New York," Joe said. Harry gave an exaggerated salute and then bowed to us.

And all of it—the potbellied guy singing, the dim lights, the doughnuts under glass, the rain-streaked window, Harry the delivery guy—I'd seen it all before, exactly like this. Déjà vu. At that moment, I heard this unbidden voice say: Home.

Though the rain didn't let up all night, a cabbie came into the coffee shop, and Joe told him about our predicament. He dropped us off at the hotel on his way home. Wouldn't take our money. I remember he was Irish, he had four-leaf-clover kitsch all over his car, and everyone called him Peppermint Paddy because his name was Patrick and he gave all his passengers a miniature York peppermint patty when they paid their fare.

It had been years since I'd been to Two Joes. The closer

I got to the Two Joes corner, the more my heart beat. By the time we got to Sixth Avenue, I was craning my neck out the cab window, looking ahead for the Two Joes sign.

When we were ten feet away, I realized I had made a terrible mistake. At that point, I couldn't really see the sign yet, but I could see an unfamiliar light coming from the storefront. Two Joes had a dimmish, warm glow. Up ahead was a bright fluorescent glow. For a moment, I wanted to turn around and bolt. I had to force myself to go towards the disturbing, unfamiliar brightness and face the truth.

Two Joes was gone.

In its place was a generic, ultramodern pizza place. The old Coke sign had been replaced by a gleaming, backlit sign in red, white, and green, the colors of the Italian flag, under which were the words "Open 24 Hours" in neon. Everything was gone—the booths, the lunch counter, the little jukeboxes, the potbellied waiters. Inside 37th Street Pizza (brilliant name), two young guys were standing idly behind the counter while one young man in very baggy pants ate a slice and glowered at the floor. It was so boring.

I turned and walked away a few feet, and abruptly I started bawling. Loudly, and I couldn't stop. I had no tissues on me, and my nose was running. I could barely see anything through the milky glaze of tears as I ran into a deli, plopped a dollar down, and asked through sobs for some tissues. The stunned guy behind the counter, who was just a flesh-colored blob with dark hair to me, gave me a whole box of tissues. With Claire and Tamayo following me and saying things I couldn't hear over the sound of my own bawling, I tore out of the store, pulling tissues out of the big box and blowing my nose as I stumbled down the street.

I plopped myself down on a curb in front of the pizza place.

Two Joes was one of the last personal landmarks left
from my first trip to New York. Over the years, I'd lost a
lot of them—the old Abbey Victoria Hotel was torn down,
Jimmy Ryan's jazz joint on 52nd Street had closed, the
Malabar Disco was a strip joint now, the Brass Rail was
gone—and now Two Joes. And there were only about a
half-dozen old-style Checker Cabs still trawling the streets
for fares. All of a sudden, I missed them terribly.

Two Joes, the one place that could always be relied on
to bring on that delicious feeling of déjà vu . . . gone,
because the city needed one more mediocre pizzeria, I
thought.

How unfamiliar the city looked to me now. I couldn't
remember anything. I felt like one of Homer's lotus-eaters
in the *Odyssey*, who ate sweet lotus fruit on a strange island
and forgot about the past, forgot about home, just wanted
to stay and eat sweet lotus fruit with the natives.

Somehow, Claire's voice broke through. "Robin, can you
talk about it?"

It took me a moment to spit it out.

"My whole life here was built on an illusion. My best
friend wasn't my best friend. I wasn't squired around by a
rich, sophisticated man and his friends, I didn't dazzle fashionable people who, won over by my natural charm, gave
me free stuff. I was squired around by a gangster, who on
at least one occasion *bought* me a date with a male pros-
titute, and whose mere appearance in a designer showroom
caused people to fearfully dish out free stuff.

"And the Saudi prince and the Finnish mogul Julie and
I danced with, they were probably just a couple of guys
from Queens trying to impress us.

"Frankie the Fish did a turn as a procurer. Just like the
white-slavers my Aunt Maureen warned me about before
I came to New York. God, is she going to enjoy this."

Tamayo was laughing.

"It's even better that you were squired around by gangsters," Tamayo said. "Rich guys are a dime a dozen in this town. But gangsters—that's an adventure."

Then I started laughing and crying, alternately.

"And we are all free women on a great adventure," I said, quoting one of Tamayo's favorite expressions.

"Oh, I've revised that," she said. "I'm a struggling demigoddess on a great adventure. Ha! Tell me again how you tried to beat that Perrugia sister with her own granny."

Just then, a cab pulled up and the driver hopped out and ran past us into the all-night pizzeria, where he slapped two bucks on the counter, asked for something, then ran into the bathroom for patrons only. A few minutes later he came out, much becalmed, and almost walked out without his pizza, which was not his priority. But then the guy behind the counter called out to him, "Hey, man, your slice." Another pizza guy took it, steaming hot, out of the oven and slapped it onto a plate. The cabbie seemed happily surprised to remember the slice, and picked it up from the counter, walking out as content as I've seen a man in quite a while. He'd had a good pee, and he was eating a nice hot slice of pizza.

Tamayo, Claire, and I all looked at each other. We laughed.

"Even though Two Joes is gone," Claire said, "what it represents is still here."

"What?"

"You didn't fall in love with the city because of those rich mobsters. Maybe they helped it along. But it was that déjà vu you had here that first night. If you hadn't met those guys, hadn't got all that free stuff, it wouldn't have mattered. You would have ended up here anyway. I know it."

"You belong here. In New York, you can be as weird as you are, and it hardly matters," Tamayo said.

"Funny that we all had cooties as kids," Claire said.

"Hilarious," I said.

"Geeks and nerds are cool now, you know? Even models have been rebelling. Did you see the last Prada show? No makeup, models slouching, walking gracelessly with stringy hair. It's like revenge of the cootie girls. Geek chic is in. It's the new model of beauty, trying not to look conventionally beautiful."

"If only the models would rebel a little more and put on some weight," I said.

The sun was up. Claire said, "Let's go to Ol' Devil Moon for a Southern breakfast. Mmmm. Grits. And you meat-eating thugs can have eggs and biscuits with pork-chop gravy. It's in your neighborhood, Robin."

"Claire, I love you. I love my girlfriends. But I've had enough sisterhood for a while. You know what I need right now?"

"A man."

"Yeah. There's something about men, you know? I can't put my finger on it. Whenever I try to name it, I can think of a bunch of women with the same quality."

"It's called a penis, Robin," Tamayo said.

"Besides that. There's something a good man has, some mysterious thing. . . ."

"Yeah, she needs a man," Claire said to Tamayo.

"But which man?" Tamayo said.

Oh, shit.

Tamayo said, "Well, we'll go downtown with you."

"You want to go to Madison Avenue with me later?" Claire asked Tamayo. "Those Tommy Mathis paintings I bought Monday? They're framed and ready for pickup today."

"Okay. We could get Susan Brave's shower present today too. Robin, you want to go in on a present for Susan's bridal shower?"

"What are you guys getting for her?"

"It's great. Well, you'll probably find something wrong with it. . . ."

Claire broke in. "One of those mechanical toilet seats. You push a button and it goes up, and then it automatically goes down when the toilet is flushed. So Susan and her husband won't ever have to worry about him leaving the seat up."

"Mechanical toilet seat. Uh-oh," I said.

"What's the problem with a mechanical toilet seat?" Tamayo asked.

"An ugly accident waiting to happen."

"How so?"

"A mechanical malfunction, a short circuit, and the toilet seat could go berserk. Some poor sod taking a crap could find himself hammered into the wall like a pancake," I explained.

"You know, I never did get that, why women complain about the toilet seat being up," Tamayo said. "After you've fallen into the bowl once, you learn not to do it the next time. You turn on the light in the bathroom, you check to make sure the seat is down, and before you leave, you put it up out of consideration for the man in your life. Or men, as the case may be. But I thought it was a funny gift. It was either that or the six-pack of Hungarian singing condoms."

"Jeez, I was thinking of giving her a gift certificate for a facial, or maybe some Tupperware."

"Tupperware, Robin?"

"That's what we always did back home. China and fancy stuff for the wedding, practical stuff at the shower."

"Tupperware is great," Tamayo said.

"It really is," Claire agreed.

"But Susan won't want Tupperware. The *old* Susan maybe, but the new Susan would much rather get the Hungarian singing condoms."

The old Susan was a nebbishy doormat to Dr. Solange Stevenson. The new Susan was a happy, confident producer at ABC, about to marry a cute doctor. Though assertiveness training and therapy helped, what really turned her around was Prozac. Made ya think.

"So what do the condoms sing?" I asked.

"Huh? Oh, there are three instrumentals, 'William Tell' Overture, Beethoven's 'Ode to Joy,' something else, and then a couple of pop songs with vocals—I can't remember what they are," Tamayo said. "The way it works is, there's a microchip at the base of the condom, which is coated with heat-sensitive stuff. When the body heat rises, the condom sings. You can't see a safety problem with those, can you?"

"Safety, no. But opportunities for pranks at the factory level . . . Instead of programming it to sing, programming it to say, 'Hey! Who turned out the lights?' "

"Or 'Remember the Alamo!' "

"Do they sing in Hungarian, Magyar, whatever it is?"

"I don't know."

"That would be scary, if the woman didn't know it was a singing condom, and then all of a sudden, during penetration, her partner's penis started singing in Hungarian. That could conceivably cause a heart attack."

"But no safety problems with Tupperware?" Claire said.

"No. Wait. You could put someone's eye out with the thing inside the lettuce crisper, and you could get cut up pretty badly if you got a finger caught in the salad spinner, but other than that . . ."

"Robin, it's amazing that you ever leave your bed," Tamayo said. She turned to Claire and said, "Do you want to go with me to visit my Grandma Scheinman on Long Island tomorrow?"

"Okay," Claire said. On they went, making plans. I tried to warn them that, as the old saying goes, when people make plans, God laughs. Or cries. I always get those two confused.

"Do you guys know the playmate song?" Tamayo asked.

We both looked at her, not sure what she was talking about.

"Playmate, come out and play with me, and bring your dollies three, climb up my apple tree, holler down my rain barrel, slide down my cellar door, and we'll be jolly friends forever more," she sang.

"She couldn't come out and play, it was a lovely day, with a tear in her eye, I heard her sigh, and then I heard her say," Claire chimed in.

"Playmate, I can't come play with you, my dolly's got the flu, boo hoo hoo hoo hoo hoo. Ain't got no rain barrel, ain't got no cellar door, but we'll be jolly friends, forever more," Tamayo sang.

She especially liked the part, "My dolly's got the flu, boo hoo hoo hoo hoo hoo." She also sang the variation, "She might throw up on you," over and over as we walked down Fifth Avenue, looking for a taxi.

I still had one crappy decision to make, Mike or Eric. But then I realized I'd made that decision, when my future flashed in front of my eyes and I saw myself with Mike, for the weekend at least. When I got home, I saw those cheesy Mecca souvenirs, and it confirmed my decision. Still, it was hard, because Eric was important to me, and incredibly sexy, and it meant slamming another door on the past. He was my transitional man. But that transition was over.

Louise Bryant was at the window. I opened it and she came in, looked up at me, and then walked over to her food dish.

"Had a good night, did you?" I asked her. I took her silence for a yes.

After I fed her, I collapsed on my bed in my clothes. I'd been going on adrenaline and a senior-citizen megavitamin all night, and now I felt like every cell in my body had been drained of life force. I slept for about an hour, and Eric called. I told him I couldn't see him. He was distressingly okay about it.

I fell asleep again. The next time I awoke, Mike was there, leaning over me, kissing my eyelids. I wasn't tired anymore. I pulled him down to me and we mated in the most unholy ways. Nearly dying is a great aphrodisiac. Afterwards, I was about to go back to sleep when the cops came. Local cops, NYPD. They wanted to speak to me about a stolen taxicab.

❂ EPILOGUE ❂

THERE'S A CULTURAL GROUP, Native American, East Timorese, something like that, who believe there comes a point in the middle of your life when you meet your own ghost. You might not recognize your ghost, but how you treat it, the lessons you learn, determines how the rest of your life will turn out.

Something like that. When I read about it, I didn't know it was going to come in handy one day, and so I didn't pay as much attention as I should have. But that's true of a lot of things in life, little things at the time that turn out to be huge things later. If only you'd known back then.

Anyway, I think that's kinda what happened to me on Halloween.

Because of cooties, I had the distinction of having an actor play me on an episode of "America's Most Wanted." More directly, it was because Julie Goomey got away with forty million of the Perrugia family's closest friends. But as I explained earlier, cooties were at the bottom of all this. If it weren't for the cooties, Julie and I wouldn't have bonded, my self-esteem would have been higher, I wouldn't have let Chuck boss me around, and I would have spent spring break '79 frying, drunk, on a beach somewhere instead of with mobsters in New York.

The actress who played Julie did a good job, but the one who played me was too short and had an annoying nasal voice. Our episode was on the special Interpol show. Since then, Julie Goomey has been sighted all over the place, but Interpol hasn't grabbed her yet. I don't think they will. She could dye her hair, wear glasses, disguise herself. With white-blond hair, she could blend in in any of the Nordic countries. With a bit of a tan, she could lose herself in India, home of the bandit queens.

Anyway, she reportedly has $40 million to keep her until the heat blows over.

Help for Kids was a legit charity she set up with Perrugia-family money and it did some good stuff, in addition to serving as one of Julie's money-laundering transit points. Meanwhile, everyone in the city is trying to find out who made an anonymous donation to the Boys and Girls Clubs of America. The note that went with it was unsigned, but I saw a picture of it in the newspaper and, guess what, I recognized the handwriting.

About a month after all this happened, I got a note from her myself, written inside a cootie catcher, with a parcel containing a costume. It was Munch's *The Scream*.

Dear Robin,
Sorry I put you through all that. I didn't know the Perrugias would grab your intern or friends, and I had arranged for the feds to meet up with you to help you out. I am having a ball. I'm painting again. Hope you're well too.
    Thanks for being such a good sport. No hard feelings, huh?

Putli Bai

Sorry. I still had hard feelings. I believed her when she said she didn't know Kathy would get caught up in it. She gave me an insurance policy, Granny, she gave us a scoop, and I guess we learned a few things along the way. On the other hand, she fucked with us and put us at incredible risk.

The voices in my head keep arguing about her. The jury

is still out. One thing I am pretty sure of, I don't think this is the last I'm going to hear of Julie Goomey in this lifetime.

The whole Perrugia clan, sans Granny, is going up the river for a very long time. Unfortunately, they still haven't found the body of Johnny "Nostrils" Chiesa, or, as I now know him, Johnny "Burgers."

It's *almost* enough to put a girl off red meat.

I guess I did learn something about recognizing the hidden menace in people. In a way, that's what I did with Granny, when I turned her into a weapon. That was resourcefulness. The bonding between my 'fro and the earring-faced boy, that was dumb luck. A happy accident. I may be living under a curse, but I seem to have enough dumb luck to keep me going.

I was not charged with grand theft auto. It seems the cursed cabbie came back a while later looking for his cab. The dispatcher I'd called hadn't understood me. The cab was eventually found in front of my building and hauled off. Once I explained the situation, they let me go.

The earring kid came forward to get his share of the reward money, which I insisted he get. He claimed he didn't have a gun, so apparently it was illegal. It's funny, I've always been for gun control, but my life was saved by a gun-law violator, and, of course, by the fact that I'd stopped relaxing my hair and gone natural. But, you know, you get older and things aren't so black and white anymore. I used to be completely against capital punishment, for example, and I still am philosophically, but I don't miss Ted Bundy. You know what I mean?

Claire's "taking the cure" on her grandmother's farm in Mississippi. Two weeks of up at dawn, slopping hogs, milking cows, and generally just living off the land might be just the ticket for her. I wouldn't mind two weeks like that myself. Except without the hogs, the cows, and the up-at-dawn stuff.

All our talk about name-callers, bullies, troublemakers, tattletales, liars, cheaters, and prideful self-righteous gossips made Claire nostalgic for that unruly playpen, Washington. So she's going back to D.C. to report, until she can get herself overseas. I know how this choice may haunt her, how, when she's down about her work, or down about her love life and her work doesn't seem to provide enough compensation for the sacrifices she's made, she might think of Jess, or her and Jess in a parallel universe, and get a little sad. But she'll get through it okay, because she has a lot of strong people in her life who love her, and she has a really big ego.

Kathy has decided to finish the semester and then go back to Florida. I don't blame her. I mean, getting kidnapped by a bunch of strange women with green wigs and guns can put anyone off a place long-term. Still, she wasn't too much the worse for wear, and I heard her telling a friend on the phone about all of it in a very excited manner, as if she was proud to have gone through it and come out of it okay. She's already turning it into a personal legend. A good outcome puts a whole different spin on events, you know?

So I figure, Kathy will be telling that story for a long time to come, and not only to a series of therapists.

Tamayo is still Tamayo. She finished her UFO screenplay and now she's writing one under contract about our Girls' Night Out. Everything is going very well for her. Somehow, she talked me into taking a torch-singing class with her. Who knows? One of us could be the next Yma Sumac, if not in this lifetime, maybe in the next one.

Phil, our super, is going to Africa, but just for a couple

of months, then he's coming back to us. I suspect it has something to do with Helen Fitkis. She's going with him, but she didn't want to go indefinitely, so they compromised. I admire them, in their seventies, going off for an adventure that way.

And get this: Tamayo's talking about taking a month and going over to Africa with Phil and Helen. To do comedy! For refugees! I've never heard of such a thing, but she says refugees need to laugh too, and it's a chance for her to work on her physical comedy, which is universal. Phil promised her she'd learn as much from the refugees as they would from her. As Tamayo figures it, somewhere out there is a funny cootie girl like her in a society that oppresses women, and she needs to find her.

("And then kill her," she jokes.)

Sally died.

While she was in the hospital, she died and was dead for all of three minutes. Although they were very long minutes, she still claims to have seen an awful lot in that brief time. And what she saw was so pleasant that, when she came to in the hospital, she screamed in horror at the faces of the doctors and nurses.

Back home and calmed down, she said that she'd been in this beautiful place, and had seen all her favorite dead relatives, plus Jesus, Buddha, Mohammed, chaos magician A. O. Spare, and her dead cat, Pie, who opened his mouth and spoke to her. He told her she had to stay on earth and fulfill her mission.

Right, Sally, gotta go, the microchip, etc.

I didn't bother to point out that all the drugs in her system might have caused her to hallucinate. Why spoil her fun?

If you want to know what heaven is like according to Sally, she'll be happy to tell you, cryptically, over a long period of time and for $50 an hour. Those on a budget can catch clues on her new public-access show on Channel 17 every Wednesday at midnight.

Maybe I make fun of her because I envy her.

Her renewed faith inspired her to fall in love again—this time with the insanely handsome man who lives upstairs, Wim Young, when he came back from doing a road show. It is, Sally declares with all confidence, True Love. She reminds me of the Countess de Lave, in the 1939 all-chick flick *The Women*, who, despite three husbands, one of whom tried to push her down a ski hill and one of whom put poison in her headache powders, never loses her faith in "*l'amour, l'amour, toujours l'amour*" (or as I know it, Le Madness).

Sally, of course, sees some kind of connection between her dream about me and the evening's outcome. If you want to make the great leap and discount the coincidence factor, I suppose you could see something in the fact that I was led by an old woman—asleep and in a wheelchair—and there was a man there whose face wasn't visible—Earring Boy. It's a stretch, but if it makes Sally feel better, what the fuck. I did have to sit her down and explain that, even if she is prophetic some of the time, I don't want to know about it. I just don't like anyone telling me the future. I'd rather be astonished, despite all the trouble this policy has gotten me into. I'm just made that way.

I did, however, let her treat me to a past-life reading by her nutty guru Sister Delia, who determined that during my human existence I had been, among other things, an uppity queen in Babylonia and later, in the tenth century, Hrotsvitha, a nun at the Abbey of Gandersheim and the prolific writer of tragedies, comedies, and histories which combined tawdry titillating spectacle with pious religious teaching. Most of Hrotsvitha's comedies feature a beleaguered virgin who wants to remain unsullied until she dies so she can arrive in heaven pure. Through all sorts of machinations, the beleaguered virgin eludes marriage for as long as she can and, if forced into marriage, escapes "defilement" by conveniently dying (clever girl). In one "comedy," the husband tries to obtain his marital prize by following his bride to her tomb, where he attempts to get amorous with the corpse. A big serpent appears and kills him. The end.

And this is one of Hrotsvitha's funnier comedies.

Most people like to hear they were someone great in a past life, and I expect past-life readers always pad the past-life résumé to play to people's egos and endear them. But this did not cheer me up. Clearly, I was working my way down the karmic ladder, from queen, to writing nun, to middle manager with little hope of advancement. At this rate, I thought, I could be a cabbie in just a few short incarnations. Or a lab rat. Made me wonder, will someone a hundred years from now consult a past-life reader and learn she was me? Will she curse or bless my name?

So I remain skeptical, because another thing I learned from this is that hindsight isn't 20/20.

Mary MacCosham and I had coffee, decided we still hated each other's guts, and haven't spoken since. The last I heard, she was in rehab back in Minnesota, trying to get her life together so she can make another attempt to get custody of her kids.

I feel sorry for Mary. What must it have been like for her, growing up with that android of a mother, never being able to live up to her mother's standards? Mary wasn't perfect, of course, and she had to feel inadequate. She knew she had secret cooties. What better way to distract attention from her cooties than to project them onto other kids?

Speaking of which . . . Dr. Solange Stevenson's book *The*

Pippi Longstocking Complex is zooming up the best-seller lists, despite rumors that the books are bound by Bangladeshi orphans. After reading her book, I've decided that I don't want to get in touch with my inner grown-up—she's a drag—but instead want to get in touch with my inner old woman. You know, figure out what kind of old woman I want to be. I know I don't want to be like Solange Stevenson, or Strip Joint Goldie, or Granny. Probably my inner old woman is just me, but older.

It took a while for me to get back into the New York groove. I felt kind of alienated from it, and yet I knew deep down I couldn't live anywhere else for any length of time. I mean, for someone like me, a cootie girl, where else is there?

I realize that the longest love affair I've ever had in my life is with this goddamned city and its goddamned citizens. When I first came here, I was infatuated. The Madness. I took a chance based on an illusion. But beneath that false love was the seed of a genuine love, true love. Now what I have for New York is like married love, kind of a warts (cooties)-and-all thing.

As for True Love between human beings, I'm revising my opinion upward in a cautious, noncommittal kind of way. I still have a couple of occasional boyfriends floating around out there, but I don't seem to have as much time for them anymore. And none of them quite measure up to Mike.

Of all my boyfriends, Mike is definitely my favorite. After the Halloween fiasco, he gave me the most interesting presents.

I love getting presents, and these are especially good.

One is a Waziri dagger, with a carved bone handle inlaid with real semiprecious aquamarine and lapis lazuli. It is gorgeous.

The other is much simpler, and yet much, much more sentimentally valuable. It's a nineteenth-century Lee Enfield rifle, hatefully captured from a dead British soldier and lovingly cared for through many generations by an Afghan family. Mike saved the present generation's lives, and the rifle was their present to him. Funny that he'd want me to have something so special to him, isn't it? I can't figure it out.

Though I've always hated guns, I love this one. It's not very efficient, not like, say, a Kalashnikov or an M-16. But it's fraught with human history and so classically formidable-looking that all one has to do is wave it to get attention.

Right, gotta go now. The microchip in my buttocks is beeping with a message from Shadow Traffic. There's a traffic jam at 34th Street and Seventh Avenue, right around Macy's—and nobody to direct it. Sounds like a job for a girl with a rifle.

But before I go, I want to leave you with the big lesson I learned from all this, said best by Yogi Berra in a commencement address in 1996:

When you come to a fork in the road, take it.

❈ ACKNOWLEDGMENTS ❈

Once again, I couldn't have finished a book without the help and support of a lot of people.

To the following people, please bend over, I'm puckering up:

All the people I thanked in my second book, *Nice Girls Finish Last*; plus

My immediate family, who allow me to twist their truths into unrecognizable fictions and outright lies to serve my plots; my funny uncles, especially my Uncles Ron, Bob, and Don, who taught me that you catch more flies with bullshit (and you catch very nice women too, judging by Aunts Pat, Jewel, and Myrna); my aunts, especially Patti Bacon Smith, aka Signed the Undersigned, who was more like a really great big sister who never ratted me out and who took me along on her undercover garden-gnome-switching operations; and my Great-Aunt and Godmother Jessie Octavia Franklin Hayter, a great dame, who gave up her cosseted Southern Belle existence to run away to the Canadian Arctic with my Great-Uncle Harry, a bush pilot, in the 1920s;

Bill Dorman, as always, you are very "greetiful," sahib; Commander Claus; Alex Dunne; Scott Griffin; Tim Moran, Paul Mougey and Roger Heaton, Matthew Poe, Harris Salat, Bruce Gillette;

My editor, Caroline White; my agent, Russell Galen; my publicist, Debbie Yautz;

Kathy Blumenstock, Carol Buckland, Nile Cmylo, Suzanne Epstein, Jean Geiger, Kyra Hicks, Big Mama Liz

Hicks, Wendy Jewell, Teresa Loftin, Martha Rodriguez, Susan Rose;

The gangs on the Prodigy Books (Mystery Books, Constant Reader, and Feminist Reader), Canada, and Black Experience BBs, DorothyL, and AOL MFTY;

George Bastable, who allows me to abuse his fine family name to get a cheap laugh, and the divine Ms. Camper;

Jack Palmer for locating and sending me a complete collection of Dana Girls mysteries;

Marigail Mathis for dressing me, Robin, and other characters, among her many contributions;

Jeff, Miriam, Lisa, and Jack at The Source in Albany;

Sleuth of Baker Street in Toronto; Booked for Murder in Madison, Wisconsin; Rue Morgue in Boulder, Colorado; Borders in Albany, New York; Partners and Crime in New York, New York (especially Maggie Griffin for sending me all the funny stuff)—Please support your independent booksellers;

Authors Jeff Abbott, John Ash, Harlan Coben, Rebecca Forster, Herbert Huncke, Jon Katz, Marlys Millhiser, Katherine Neville, Steve O'Donnell, Walter Satterthwait, Justin Scott, Arnold Weinstein;

Stanley Bard, David Bard, Jerry Weinstein, and the entire staff of the Hotel Chelsea, without whom I would have been homeless;

All the fine-looking gentlemen at the Aristocrat Deli;

The late William J. Sloane, the late Boo Radley; the late Miranda, and Demetrius.

Honor and the code of my tribe require that I now say this: Ray Fowler got me. He got me good. Ray Fowler is the practical joke king.

Temporarily.

Heh-heh-heh.